TELLING STORIES

Telling Stories

NEW ENGLISH FICTION FROM QUÉBEC

EDITED BY

Claude Lalumière

Véhicule Press

MONTRÉAL

Published with the generous assistance of The Canada Council
for the Arts, the Book Publishing Industry Development
Program of the Department of Canadian Heritage, and the
Société de développement des entreprises culturelles du
Québec (SODEC).

The publisher also appreciates the collaboration of CBC
Montreal and the Quebec Writers' Federation.

Cover design: J.W. Stewart
Set in Adobe Minion by Simon Garamond
Printed by AGMV-Marquis Inc.

CATALOGUING IN PUBLICATION DATA

Telling stories : new English stories from Quebec

ISBN 1-55065-161-7

1. Short stories, Canadian (English) – Quebec (Province)
2. Canadian fiction (English) – 20th century.
I. Lalumière, Claude

PS8329.5.Q4T45 2002   C813'.01089714   C2002-900843-3
PR9197.32.T45 2002

Published by Véhicule Press
P.O.B. 125, Place du Parc Station
Montréal, Québec H2W 2M9

www.vehiculepress.com
Distributed in Canada by General Distribution Services.

Printed in Canada on alkaline paper.

Contents

Preface

One of the real joys of working at the CBC is that we can actively encourage and support the talented, creative people within our community. Three years ago, CBC Radio and the Québec Writers' Federation got together to create a new short story competition. We didn't know who would enter, but we knew that there were English-speaking writers in Québec who would be happy to have a new outlet for their work.

It has been a real surprise, and a real pleasure, to discover the range of people the competition attracts. Over the last three years, there have been entries from around the province, from high school students as well as from senior citizens, from published authors and from those who are at a fairly early stage in their careers.

What I've especially enjoyed about this competition is being able to encourage those who are relatively new to writing – and there are many of those in this book. It's been wonderful to hear the excitement in their voices when I call and tell them they've won or are runners-up in the competition. And it's been clear, as I've worked with the winners to dramatize their stories for radio broadcast, that this excitement lasts for a while.

But what also gives me pleasure, every year, is seeing the number of people who enter. Because I really do think that winning isn't everything. And it makes me feel good to live in a place where so many people find pleasure and meaning in the act of creating.

The winning stories have all been produced and have aired on CBC Radio. But now, thanks to Simon Dardick and Vicki Marcok of Véhicule Press and to Claude Lalumière, who edited the book, these stories will also exist in print. This volume also gives us the opportunity to present for the first time the stories that garnered honourable mentions.

I hope you'll enjoy discovering what some of the new English-language writers in Québec are thinking and saying.

Katherine Gombay, CBC Radio
Executive Producer, CBC-QWF Short Story Competition

Introduction

What's Good about Contests
(From a Writer's Point of View)

Writers work alone. Yet their work, from the very moment of conception, is directed to readers. Writers need readers. No, let's be brutally frank. Writers long for readers. Unfortunately, the usual way for a short-story writer to reach those desirable creatures is through submission to magazines and to literary quarterlies, a process that can produce enough rejection slips to paper a writer's workroom. Getting published is tough. No-one will deny it. So, what do contests bring to this situation?

1. Contests say that somebody, other than the writers themselves, cares, that somebody is actually looking for good, new work.

2. Contests reach out, beyond the literati, that is beyond the writers and publishers and critics, into the community at large.

3. Contests stir the pot. They represent the opportunity for a new flavour – new kinds of writing, new styles, new language, new subjects – to come bubbling up through the layers of accepted "good writing" to surprise and excite us.

4. Contests make everyone pay attention. Our species, the biologists tell us, is fundamentally competitive, and just as we're interested to know who wins in sports and politics, whether it's the Masters in golf or an election in Montreal or in Russia, we tend to sit up and pay attention when a literary contest comes along, taking note of winning stories and their authors – and making a special effort to read their work.

5. Contests offer writers the chance to leap forward out of the crowd. Most editors and publishers pay little attention or even reject out of hand submissions from writers they've never heard

of. It's understandable; they get an overwhelming number of submissions. Furthermore, in considering submissions, they cannot help but be affected by their knowledge of who writers are and what they have already done. This is both natural and practical from their point of view. But in a contest all legitimate submissions are considered. And in the CBC-QWF contest, authors' names are not revealed to the jurors. Thus all entries are judged on an equal footing, and the oft-published, well-regarded author has no advantage over the complete unknown.

6. Contests encourage writers to write. Remember the writer working all alone in that well-papered workroom? The contest provides a deadline. Finish that story, the pesky one that you've left simmering on the back burner for months or years. Write into existence that brilliant idea you jotted down and filed away with your other ideas-for-stories. Without the contest, not all these fine stories would have been written.

7. Contests invite writers to be brave. Contests are not only about winning; they are about entering. And, believe me, it takes courage for a writer to seal up her creation, her baby, in an envelope and mail it off to strangers. But this willingness to be judged, this blind offering of a writer's best effort, this self-exposure, is an integral part of the writing life. A writer needs to take the risk. And, by the way, now and then the existence of a contest will inspire a book such as this one, an anthology of daring, sensitive, thoughtful stories by writers who have written in solitude and now, in many cases for the first time, are about to make contact with that longed-for reader, who happens to be you.

From a writer's point of view, whether we win or we don't, contests are good news.

Julie Keith,
President, Québec Writers' Federation

1999-2000

SUZANNE ALEXAKIS

Professor Hopkins Goes Swimming

He dives in.

Laps one and two.

The problem: he's invisible to the new art teacher. He doesn't have a chance unless, first, he can make her notice him. And he doesn't have all the time in the world, with retirement looming. He has tried wearing his hand-painted tie. He has considered dying his hair black, but black hair makes his nose look bigger and his cheeks fat.

The aquafitness ladies are now presenting their chorus line of asses. He'd like to swim up and goose them, but couldn't get away with it. *Georgie Porgie, pudding 'n' pie, goosed the girls and made them cry.*

Laps three and four.

He could wander into the teacher's lounge carrying a copy of the art history journal where he once had an article published. A tad obvious. Or dress in his 1970s musketeer-style shirt to appear daring? Flair, my dear. And he'd be fencing with wisecracks all day. Perhaps, he should try solicitude: "One of the worst things about a new job is you don't know any good spots for lunch. Have you tried the little restaurant on the corner of Fort Street? It's really quite good."

"No, I haven't."

"Well, I'm headed down there today, if you'd like to join me."

"I'm afraid I don't have time today. I'm meeting with a student at half-past twelve."

Strikeout. A student, at lunchtime? Probably some black-haired youth with a musketeer-style shirt who's closer to her own age.

Laps five and six.

He has failed to intrigue her. At the staff meeting he said nothing. Elbows on table, chin resting on the apex of his hands, he appeared to ponder, while looking continuously in her direction. It's hard to ignore this. Why did she? She was too excited about the art show she is organizing and the enthusiasm it's generating among students. Her first position in a CEGEP. Aspiring and inspiring. Even flop-head Frank wants to help her, and he hasn't volunteered for anything in six years.

Laps seven and eight.

Enthusiasm. A sparkling drink that makes you feel all fizzy. The aquafitness ladies are frothing up the pool with their kicking calves. He fights against the lateral action and waits at the other end of the pool for things to die down.

An idea! But how to make her come to it herself?

"I wonder, are any of your students incorporating text into their artwork? A couple of my writing students are quite interested in that sort of thing."

"That would be an interesting area to explore. Do you think some of your writers would like to come to a couple of our workshops for a creative exchange?"

Bingo. Creative exchange, that's what he's after. He'll tell his students, "an exciting opportunity. Many famous collaborations." That ought to stimulate some interest among the future literati in his class. And just to make sure he'll make it count for an essay.

Laps nine and ten.

Middleton is in the pool.

"Doesn't get any easier, does it, Tompkins?"

"Just takes a little perseverance," he says, leaving Middleton resting at the end of the pool. Two years, and he still can't get his name right. Hopkins, not Tompkins; it's Hopkins. It appears in every school document as such and is glued onto his door. Middleton is a hollow-brained fool.

He is jealous of Middleton's good looks.

The aquawomen are now plunging little green barbells in the water. He hears the glug, glug, glug.

Laps eleven and twelve.

Make an effort. If he's to hold her in his once-more illustrious arms. Kick and pull. He's swamping Middleton in his wake.

She is pointing to an impressive piece of collaboration between their students. Her hands dance gracefully in front of the canvas as she illustrates its features. "Ah yes," he says and steps in closer. He sees how the rhythm of the painting mirrors that of the text. She turns to look at him in appreciation of this thought.

"Yes," she says. "Here, the artist wanted the words to be like branches in front of a window."

"Words can be so many things," he says, "a bridge, an embrace."

He glides past the aquawomen, who are now floating on their backs.

Laps thirteen and fourteen.

Breaststroke. He is swimming over her body. Lightly. She fills the space between his arms. She encircles his waist. Her fingers cup his scrotum, enter the crevices gently as water. Her hands swirl between and down the backs of his legs. His hands are circling her breasts. Somehow they are large enough to fill the span of his swim stroke.

The aquawomen have paused between exercises. They're looking in his direction. No privacy in this pool.

Laps fifteen and sixteen.

Time for some crawl. He's still in pretty good shape. After all that wallowing foreplay, he'll do a smart beeline and keep going strong all the way to the end. Straight back, springboard spine, keep going, past the halfway mark. Keep the energy up, smooth movement, lungs strong, gentle thrust. There's the wall, almost there, and glide, glide in on the final burst. Touch the concrete and hold, just for a moment, then elastically turn and start back in a slow, graceful stroke, savouring the infusion of vigour. He pauses at the other end of the pool, pleasantly flushed, and embraces the aquawomen with his gaze.

Laps seventeen and eighteen.

He's hungry. Four more laps, and he'll have the pretty deli girl make him a sandwich with lots of mayonnaise, lots of meat, and some juicy sliced tomato. He's taking it easy now. He watches the aquafitness class cooling down. The plump women in their shiny swimsuits. Ample breasts and legs. They look relaxed now too. Among them is one whom he has visited. Little excuses once brought him to Helen Macpherson's door. The second time she gave him tea and homemade buns. And the third time she gave him everything, in the spare room, halfway through a tour of the house. Why did he stop going to see Helen? It was getting complicated. She called his home a few times. Friends with his wife's younger sister.

Laps nineteen and twenty.

The women are off to the changing room. It will be full of flesh and gossip for fifteen minutes. They all keep secrets from each other though.

In the men's room, Middleton will be soaping himself up in the shower.

"Gets the old blood pumping, eh, Tompkins."

"Have to keep fit for the ladies," he'll say in a way intended to make Middleton feel he's missing something. Middleton's too dumb to get bored. But Middleton is young.

He, on the other hand, has lost much ground to the relentless temporal treadmill. And so he must look for ways to cock up the mechanism now and again, before it crunches his bones to fine powder.

Twenty laps, and he rises like Poseidon from the pool. Perhaps he should wait outside for Helen Macpherson. But the women take so damn long to change.

Pneumonia

When she finally did get pneumonia it was on a Tuesday afternoon, just after her son's recorder recital at school. She felt it first in her arm, which was not at all what she had expected. For some reason, she had understood that pneumonia began in the lungs, but, no, that was not true the doctor later told her; it always begins in the arm. Her arm started to twitch on the drive home from school, and soon it began to twitch so badly that she lost control of the car. The car slammed into a cement mixer, the side of the car bouncing off the metal of the machine and slamming back into it again. All three of her children were killed, and when to she went to the police inquiry they told her it was a miracle that she was alive, that the twitching in her arm made the car slam into the cement mixer on such an angle that she remained untouched. The pneumonia, the doctor later testified, had saved her life.

There were fish, and there were fish ornaments hanging on the walls, papier mâché and metal, origami and plastic, all colours, all sizes, some blue, some green, some the size of a man's hand, others the size of a child's foot. Fish cushions crushed in a chair, breathing fish circling in an aquarium. This doctor was a man. When the doctor said , "How are we today?" she did not like him, because he assumed that the two of them were in this together. She could not reply but instead looked at the bubbles in the aquarium that sounded like someone sucking the last bit of a milkshake.

For an hour she sat with this doctor, a psychiatrist, who told her how he had once helped coach his daughter's gymnastic team. The girls were four, and their only goal for the day's lesson was to walk across a beam on the floor, about as high as a curb next to a street. Before each girl went across he'd tell them, "You can do it, go," and they would go, some tripping, some falling, but for the most part, balancing. Then he told every second girl, "Don't fall, don't fall," and every second girl fell. Do you know why they fell, he wanted to know from her, and she didn't want to answer, she didn't want him to either, she didn't want to know, and he said, "It's because I told them not to. Thinking negative produces negative. Let's try to remember that for our next session." His voice was gentle and prodding, and she thought that he felt self-important or that he had actually helped her. She said nothing and refused to leave. She liked the anxiousness in his voice when he called to the receptionist, "Ah, Sylvie, we've got a bit of a problem here." The doctor didn't want to cause a scene, so he saw the rest of the day's patients in another office. She sat in the fish room for the rest of the day thinking, "What kind of person would make little girls fall?"

In her dreams, pneumonia came to her in waves, with a sobbing lung, an inflamed bronchus. Pneumonia burned her breath, blazed through her throat. She felt as though she had swallowed a match, had mistaken the Drano for milk. The flames consumed her lungs, moved up her throat; the flames were in her mouth, her fillings melted. She choked, and her chest collapsed. She could not breathe, the air burned; pneumonia tortured her, it killed her in her sleep. At the end of one dream, she'd slashed her own throat to end the pain, then pulled out the bloody knife. "I've done it," she dreamed herself thinking before Corinne jumped on her, saying, "Mum, you promised Eggos today."

Now she could not dream, and it was embarrassing in the way it was embarrassing when they asked for a urine sample and she couldn't make herself go. "Just think of waterfalls, of flowing rivers, of streams." The nurse was standing with her foot in the bathroom door (her broad leg looked like a tree stump with overgrown roots), asking if turning on the tap would help.

She could not relax, she could not go, she could not dream of pneumonia now that she had it. She could not dream of her children, now that they were gone.

She did not suffer in the hospital as much as she had suffered in her dreams; pneumonia was not so disabling. In the hospital they gave her antidepressants, sleeping pills, and green Jell-O. In the hospital she had her own room, with bars on the windows in case she tried to get out, without light fixtures in case she wanted to hang herself. For the first few weeks after the accident her wrist (but not the broken one) and ankles were tied to the bed so that she wouldn't hurt herself and the room slowed down, and before she slept her empty sleep she thought, "What more could it hurt?"

The word pneumonia was hard to read. She remembered the day she first learned to spell it, that quiet P that snuck up on her in tests or in reading equivalencies given by the government. She remembered the numbness of her throat, the pounding of her heart in her head when she realized, "Here is a word that cannot be sounded out."

When she was young, her father was the manager of a picture-frame factory. On the second Sunday of every May, every year, he had the entire family dress up, and they all went down to the riverbank and had their picture taken. These were to be put in the frames, the frames made in the factory, as sample photographs; her father knew how to sell a frame: it helped to show a happy, well-dressed family.

The picture was not real, it came with the frame, and when another family bought it they put their own picture in. Her father knew how to do it; her father knew how to show a happy, well-dressed family. Her father beat both her eyes with the bottom of his shoe, with his hands, his right hand on the shoe, his left hand holding her down. The next day she went to school with two black eyes, and no-one asked; they knew to say nothing, that there was no sound for it, like the P on the front of pneumonia.

She once dreamed that she didn't know what to make for supper, so she took the paring knife (because it was smaller and easier to handle) and began to cut out her heart, starting just below her sternum and moving up between her breasts, which had begun to slacken since she'd switched Lyla to formula. She continued to cut until she could get a good grip on her sternum, pulling the bone up, making it crack, small bones flying as they did when she filleted the fish her father caught. With the sternum out of her way, she easily slid the knife under the values and cut. There was not much blood, but her heart was a mess; it was a shapeless thing; it was lumpy, throbbing. She washed it and put it in the oven at 375°F for forty-five minutes. She boiled rice and steamed carrots. When her children asked, she would tell them the red stuff was ketchup.

In her dreams, the pneumonia spread. After the dream in which she fed her children her heart, she no longer dreamed of pneumonia in her lungs. Pneumonia had spread to her brain, an infectious fever that overtook her senses. Now it was her head that burned, her mind that melted. She dreamed that her children were reaching out to her, but pretended that she did not recognize them. If she did, they would surely be killed. So she sent them all away and found a sturdy beam in the basement, and a rope, and a box to stand on, and she made a loop and a sheep knot because she didn't know how to make a proper knot, and she put the rope around her neck, and she kicked the box away, feeling a burning up her spine and an explosion in her head, wanting only release, only calm and nothingness. She felt herself twitch and kick. She waited for the wash of quiet, but it never came: the pneumonia had settled in her brain, had infected it, had scorched every nerve ending, every important connector.

"What were her reasons for living?" the doctor needed to know. It was the fish doctor, the brain monger. "Look deep inside yourself," he talked like the radio, "what do you see?"

She saw charred fibres, blackened tubes; she saw an empty space, still smoldering, in ruins, where her lungs and heart used to be. She saw disconnected values like melted wires, the dripping mess of a gutted house. She saw all of this but told him nothing; she let him talk to himself, let him fill the void between them with unimportant words.

"At least blink if you can hear me," he spoke to her as if she didn't understand English. Do this, he showed her, flipping his eyelids down, then up, his eyeballs rolling so much that all she saw was white. She did nothing but watch the glazed whites of his eyelids quiver. His tie had little tropical fish on it. They were yellow and blue; the water was a darker blue.

In the hospital, there were crafts; she could glue pieces of felt together to make a shape. To make a mouse, it took one large grey teardrop for the body and two small black teardrops for the ears. She glued on a tail that was a string of black yarn. The pieces were cut for her: they wouldn't let her have scissors. Her food was cut for her, too, but she wouldn't eat. For the most of the day she sat in a chair in her room, looked at the flower pattern of her slippers, followed the leaves and the petals until they put her in bed. She wouldn't open her mouth, she would no longer swallow pills. The doctor gave her a needle until her arm twitched, and she felt the veins open up, and her arm seemed to float, on its own, as if it were a helium balloon without a string. The feeling spread, from her arm to her spine to her head; she saw very clearly the room and the flowers at her bedside, the yellow painted walls; these moments were her most lucid. She remembered why she was there. Today she remembered her reasons for living: when her son practiced the recorder in the kitchen, how she had counted one-two-three-four for him and swayed the baby on her hip, twirled Corinne under her arm and heard her shout, "Mum, is my skirt a tulip or a daffodil when it opens when I turn?"

NICK CARPENTER

Staring at Miracles

So I begin to sing.

And when I'm finished, the whole class is staring. Just staring at me. Someone's jawbreaker falls out of his mouth. The teacher is crying. But mostly she's just staring at me. Like the rest of them. That's when I know I'm good at "O Canada."

There's no echo. It's not like a church or an arena or a canyon. It's like a grade 1 classroom with the sound of 29 pairs of eyes blinking and one jawbreaker bouncing on linoleum.

Once, in a barn, I looked at a little cow coming out of a big cow. My mother held my hand and told me I was allowed to stare at miracles. I stand in the middle of the classroom, and I wonder if I am a miracle.

I am so good at "O Canada" that the teacher tells everybody to get their crayons out and celebrate. We draw black mountains and blue fish and yellow suns that grin from the top of our foolscaps. At recess, my teacher marches me to Ms. Hark, the school principal, and makes me sing "O Canada" again.

Now Ms. Hark is crying.

They both take me to Mr. Bartholomew, who is not only a man but a gym teacher. I sing it again. My voice fills the gymnasium. This time there is an echo and the song sounds even more important than I thought it was. Mr. Bartholomew's chest collapses. We leave him shuddering on a medicine ball and close the door behind us.

In the hall, Ms. Hark asks me who taught me to sing like that. And I don't say anything ... because I don't understand her. Because, you see, I only arrived in Canada one week ago and the only English or French words I know are the words to "O Canada."

I think she's asking me to sing it again. So I do. And, one by one, classroom doors open, and the hall fills with hundreds of huge, wet, staring Canadian eyes. I wonder if I am a miracle.

At lunch, two boys get into a fight. The yard monitor makes me sing "O Canada." The boys not only stop fighting, they become best friends. By the end of lunch, they're trading hockey cards.

That afternoon, Ms. Hark calls my mother at home. My mother calls my father at work. My father calls a talent agent downtown. The talent agent calls a producer in Toronto. The producer calls my father that night during dessert. My father calls me into the next room and hands me the telephone. I sing "Oh Canada."

The next evening, during dessert, I am in Toronto, singing "O Canada" in front of 20,000 people. I am at a place called The Gardens of the Maple Leaf. When I finish, a cheer is raised that pushes all the air out of my body ...

My friends catch me. My old friends. I have no idea how they knew that all the air would leave my body. But there they are. A hundred hands on my back. A colour I know. A language I can answer. And I'm pushed back to my feet. They ask me what Canada is like. I tell them there's a song I'd like to teach them. A Canadian song. And then my grandparents are there. My cousins. The shopkeeper. The bicycle man with dust from the roads. A farmer with muddy hands and fruit that I thought I would never smell again. I tell them there is a beautiful song they absolutely must hear. But my grandmother asks me where my air is. "You cannot dance without air." "Not a dance," I correct her, "a song." And I sing it. But she stops me and tells me to dance. "I want to sing." I say. "Dance!" she shouts. "But I have to sing the song!" I scream.

And then ... they are gone. A microphone. The Maple Leaf. 20,000 people. Ice. A game. A paper cup in my hands. My mother's voice: "Breathe." I breathe. "Drink." I drink from the paper cup. My father's voice: "Smile." I smile. Someone takes my picture.

It is amazing how light "O Canada" is. I begin to take it wherever I go. Sports halls, conference halls, churches and museums. I sing "O Canada" on boats, on television, on radio, and once, on the first of April, on helium.

I sing for ambassadors and presidents. I'm booked for the Pope, but he gets food poisoning.

When I am nine, I sing "O Canada" for my own mother, except it's her funeral so I don't think she hears it. I sing it at legion halls, at rallies, at dog-shows, at book launches and rocket launches. Whenever a ribbon is cut in this country, I sing.

I sing "O Canada" for my own twelfth birthday. I open my present. A sweatshirt with a maple leaf. Everyone in the stadium is crying. I wonder if I am a miracle.

When I am fourteen, I sing "O Canada" to a 21-gun salute. Long coats and long faces with tears in their eyes. Me with blood in my ear. At the hospital, they tell my left eardrum that my right eardrum has been punctured.

When I am sixteen, I sing in a wheat field in January, in jeans and a cowboy hat. A twelve-ton granite Indian gets a sheet pulled off him. I see everybody wipe tears on the sleeves of their parkas. As my sore throat turns into pneumonia, I come to the conclusion that I am a miracle.

When I am eighteen, I sing for a pocket of peacekeepers. I'm in a country having difficulty coming up with a national anthem. A few of its citizens send their jealousy disguised as a mortar shell. My armoured car is turned over. I sing that evening. Seeing so many soldiers cry more than makes up for my separated shoulder.

When I am nineteen, I sing "O Canada" eight times in a row because Prince Charles is late. On the last verse of the eighth time, I start to cry. And all the tears leave my body ...

My friends find me. My old friends. I have no idea how they knew that all the tears would leave my body. But there they are. A hundred hands on my back. A colour I know. A language I can answer. They ask me what Canada is like. I tell them there's a landscape I'd like to draw for them. A Canadian landscape. And then my grandparents are there. My aunt with crooked hips. The sailor with three teeth made from the hilt of his sword. The shopkeeper with a bag of nuts I thought I would never taste again. I tell them there is a beautiful landscape they absolutely must see. My grandfather asks me why my fingernails are so long and tells me I can't eat nuts with long nails. "I'll eat them later." I say, "I want to draw you a picture." And I draw it. With a branch in the dry, warm road. Mountains, fish, sun. My grandfather stops me and orders me to eat. "Look at my pictures!" I say. He looks at it. He asks me why I have drawn a circle around the mountains, the fish, and the sun. "That's the window of the airplane," I say.

And then ... they're gone. A reception hall. Prince Charles. I am taken into the next room so that he will not see me. It takes me all night and half the next day to stop crying.

In the airplane, my father is pleased to announce to me that I am feeling better.

A new school. Very much like the old one. I think of Ms. Hark. I think of Mr. Bartholomew sobbing on the medicine ball. I think of the fight I stopped in the schoolyard. The two boys who became best friends. I remember hearing that one had gone on to do History at Harvard and the other had burnt down a church.

In fact, the last thing I actually think about is where I am.

I open my mouth and out comes "O Canada." Flawless. As always. When I am finished, I wait, as always, for the tears and the thunder. And, as always, a second of silence hovers to consecrate the miracle. But the second turns into a moment. And the moment turns into a nightmare.

My mind snaps to attention, and my gut somersaults. I have sung "O Canada" in the wrong language. The last note has emptied my lungs. I draw in my breath slowly. Like a hare being sniffed by a wolf. A silence to kill all song. I stumble off my podium. To the left there are no doors. To the right, only windows. Before me, a sea of Canadian eyes. So dry that I can hear their eyelids scrape when they blink.

And then, closer, directly in front of me. One face. Just one face. Dry eyes. Full of injury. A mouth full of hatred. A flash and my head snaps backwards. Another flash and my spine curls forwards. All the blood leaves my body ...

My friends catch me. I don't know how they knew the blood would leave my body. But there they are. A hundred hands on my back. A colour I know. A language I can answer. And I am pushed to my feet. They ask me what Canada is like. I tell them there is a story I'd like to tell them. A Canadian story. And then my grandparents are there. My uncle with his traps and nine fingers and a carcass from the forest. The shopkeeper with a bag of nutshells. The farmer from the barn carrying the little cow that had died only hours after coming out of the big cow. A look on his face I had hoped never to see again. I tell them there is a story that they absolutely must hear. My grandparents ask me where my blood is. "You can't pray without blood." "Not a prayer," I correct them, "a story." And I begin my story. But they stop me and order me to find my blood. "My story!" I say. "Your blood!" they shout, "Your blood, or you're lost!" "I don't need my blood! I'm a miracle!"

And then ... they're gone. A little school. A podium. A lake of dry eyes. Staring at me. I get up and walk right through them, through the door and out toward the black mountains and the yellow sun.

EMMA ROBERTS

Heaven Tate

My mother thinks I'm a banker.

My girlfriend Janine works at the TD downtown. Whenever my mother calls, Janine picks up and says, "Sorry, Candy. Dave's in a conference" or "Sorry, Candy. Dave's in Copenhagen," and has a conversation with her instead. Janine has three kids, and talking to her seems to slake Candy's thirst for grandchildren. Candy doesn't call me at home. She's lived in Florida since Dad died. Doesn't seem to annoy her much that I've never answered the phone in eleven years.

My bank statement this month was a long stare into a poor future. Maybe it's time to dry clean the old nine-to-five pinstripe suit. I'm beginning to think Janine has the right idea.

I got the call on Tuesday night. I could tell she was a kid, but how much of a kid wasn't clear. My guess was twelve. Second call came the next evening. She disguised her voice. Third call the evening after that; and the fourth, two minutes later: "Look. Will you at least talk to me? It's not for me. It's for my Auntie Louanne and she's turning forty. Hear that? FORTY. LEGAL!"

I looked at my bank account. I called.

Sandra's one of those children who makes a business of her life before she has to. The word that comes to mind is *efficient*.

"How much for flowers, wine, dinner, dancing, a walk in the moonlight, and twenty minutes of necking on the couch?"

It took me a moment to tally it up. "Flat rate is $110 an hour. Average date lasts four hours, with a fifteen minute slap and tickle session as a bonus. Daisies, an uninspiring red, dinner and dancing take place in the same location, you're looking at five twenty plus cab fare and incidentals."

"Incidentals?"

"Cigarettes, mood enhancers, condoms."

"She won't go that far."

I reminded myself this was a twelve year old. "If she does it's negotiable. Depending on the act." Something went "tap-tap-tap" in the background. "What is that, a keyboard?"

"Calculator. What if you like her?" Sandra asked, "Can I get a discount?"

I laughed and hung up.

The kid called back the next day and offered me six hundred plus gas. She lived out in the boonies. I explained that I would arrive at seven-thirty and depart at eleven-thirty and anything over that was time and a half.

"That'll be enough," she said.

My fault for not asking. I needed the money. I'm a professional. But I can get buttered up. I think I admired her pluck. I'll never be able to explain why I didn't ask the crucial question: why can't Auntie Louanne get a date on her own?

Driving out to the farm the muffler finally went. I bobbed along like an overweight bumblebee, realizing I should have married a rich widow. Janine says I'd make more money if I swung both ways, but I like the idea of being an exclusively female service. Truth is, you can't make a living on romance anymore. It's a cynical world.

I was greeted by three massive Dobermans. A small girl with braids ran up to me. She smiled. Her braces glinted in the barn's motion detector.

"Supper's almost ready," she grinned.

There are moments in life when time freezes in horror. I walked in that room, and the clock turned to stone. I glimpsed three women sitting very close together on the couch. Then, as my eyes absorbed the truth, the three melded into one. A twenty-year/two-pack-a-day voice muttered, "You didn't tell him. Did you?"

Thirty-three years ago Candy called me David. David Allen Pritchard. A clean upstanding suburban name. I am now Heaven Tate. I chose that name for a reason. I can bring a girl so close to God, she'd have to die to one-up me. When I was nine years old, my father joked that we should hire a receptionist to handle all the calls from girls. When I was ten, my mother made the number unlisted. When I was eleven, my fourteen-year-old babysitter made a man out of me. By the time I turned twenty-one, I had had one hundred girlfriends. It's true. I counted. I'm a natural for this business. This is what I knew about myself walking into that sitting room. And then as I was walking out, I said to myself, "I learned something new tonight."

The bumblebee was almost at the end of the lane when the headlights caught those braces and shot sparks of light up into the country black. The kid ran left and right, determined to block my escape. I jumped out of the car, stormed up to Sandra, and grabbed her by the shoulders. I said, "Listen. God knows this is the only way she'll – but I can't."

"She weighs five hundred and seventy-six pounds."

"My condolences."

"She was only seven pounds six ounces when she was born. The doctor says her heart could power a stadium."

"I gotta go."

"I'll give you three thousand dollars."

I don't ever get personal. But here again. It was this kid I couldn't seem to find a weapon against. "Let me see the money."

She handed me a pink plastic lunchbox. A hundred and fifty twenties smiled up at me. Sandra's face made me ask, "Why is this so important to you?"

"She's never had a date. She's never had a man call her. She's never had a valentine. She's never even had a male friend. All she has is me."

Sandra stared so pleadingly I felt my skin begin to buckle. The Dobermans scratched themselves and waited for my reply. I thought about the car repairs I could now afford.

"Eleven thirty-one I'm a pumpkin," I said, as I strode back into the house.

Louanne smoked and stared. I kissed her hand. It smelled like tobacco. Her skin was igloo white. She had perfect teeth. Blue eyes.

"How much did she pay you?"

I don't like discussing money once the deal is made.

"How about a game of rummy? Do you enjoy rummy?" I attempted. Louanne lifted her hand slightly in a gesture of slow disgust.

"I risk a fracture every time I scratch my nose. I don't enjoy anything. Except sleep."

For a moment I thought about leaving again.

"This wasn't my idea," she coughed, "but my baby girl wanted to do it, so I went along with it. She thinks I'm lonely."

Sandra poked her head out of the kitchen and beckoned me over.

"I'm just waiting on the quiche," she chirped. "Why not take Louanne for a stroll out back?"

I looked at her. I knew there was no way that Louanne could walk. Sandra gave me her trademark metal smirk and walked behind the couch. She grabbed a starter cord from somewhere and yanked it. The couch had ignition. Sandra gave me the wine, an opener, two glasses, and a cheeky wink. Louanne manoeuvred out through the kitchen, and we went outside.

I never get personal. But something about these two had me intensely curious.

"Who made that for you? That couch-mobile?" I had to ask.

"Sandra." Louanne said simply, as though I were an idiot for asking. "She's a genius. She runs this place."

"You mean?"

"It's just me and her. I suppose I shouldn't tell you that. You are a stranger. But we've survived fairly well for a little elf and a beached whale. She makes me proud. Except for tonight, of course."

I looked at her. It was so hard to be businesslike. I couldn't explain the concern I had for them. I never get personal. I was feeling inhabited by a foreign entity.

"Please don't encourage me to lose weight."

"What makes you think–?"

"Let me show you the tomatoes."

She was warming up.

We motored on behind the house, and Louanne clapped her hands. Lights came on in a circle around a garden. There was every kind of vegetable, all in a magical, technicolour bloom. I opened the wine and poured a glass for Louanne.

"This was three hundred pounds ago," Louanne said as she lit a cigarette. "Two months on my hands and knees, and black flies to boot. Sandra's looking after it now. It's managed to outlive me." Louanne looked at her tomatoes. "Hello, my babies. Hello, how are you? Oh, look how beautiful you are."

Standing there in the floodlit garden I was thinking of past clients – which I never do. But on this night the faces of hundreds of women floated before me. Anxious women paying to be liked. And here was Louanne. Cooing at her tomatoes as though they were kittens. I suddenly thought – and now that I'm telling it, it sounds weirder still – what will happen to them? What will become of them? How will they survive?

I leaned across the whirring couch and kissed her.

Saturday Night

Dimitri was hiding behind the washing machine again.

Beth-Ann slipped her quarters into the slots and pushed them in. As the water filled, she dropped her clothes into the washer. She scooped detergent into her plastic measuring cup. And she ignored Dimitri. Pretended she didn't know he was there; pretended she couldn't hear him breathing behind the washing machine.

Beth-Ann sprinkled the detergent on her clothes and closed the lid. She counted her change for the dryer, for later. She told herself to stop stalling, that she could count her change upstairs, in her apartment. She told herself to hurry; she had timed her wash to start at the beginning of the nine-thirty television shows and was going to miss all of the opening sequences if she didn't hustle.

She bit the edge of her thumbnail. She reached back into the box of detergent and grabbed a little cluster of soap crystals with the tips of her fingers. She flung them casually behind the washer and walked quickly to the elevator.

There wasn't much room behind the washing machine. Dimitri's back pressed hard against the wall, and his drawn up thighs pressed hard against his stomach and chest. His arms were wrapped around his bent knees, hands clasped together. The toes of his running shoes bent backward against the machine's back panel. His neck curled forward, keeping his head from touching the black rubber water hoses. Remaining in this position for long periods of time caused Dimitri to breathe loudly.

It was dirty behind the washing machine. And dusty. Balls of lint – grey ones, yellow ones, baby-blue ones – littered the concrete floor in the small space between the machine and the wall. White paint chips were scattered like confetti. One lonely black sock, riddled with dust and lint, lay on the ground. An abandoned-looking cobweb hung between the washer and dryer, down near the floor, only a few detergent crystals snared. Behind the washing machine, Dimitri inhaled dust, and it made him wheeze quietly.

He pushed himself up, feeling the cracks in the wall pass against his back, until he was standing. He stretched his arms and neck. He twiddled his toes inside his shoes. He brushed the front of his shirt off, creating a small cloud of dust and lint and paint chips. He sidestepped to the right and came out from behind the washing machine. He crawled into the dryer and waited.

Beth-Ann returned to the basement during the commercial break between the end of the nine-thirty shows and the beginning of the ten o'clock shows. Half-hour programs were for washing, hour-long programs were for drying – the timing was impeccable. Beth-Ann had exactly three minutes and thirty seconds to go downstairs, stuff her wet clothes in the dryer, place the coins, start the machine, and dash back upstairs again. After that, she would have an hour to stretch out on the couch with a bag of vinegar chips and a bottle of Pepsi, free to flip back and forth between the worlds of warriors, barbarians, and Texas rangers. She was so intent on making it back on time that she nearly forgot about Dimitri.

But as soon as she saw the washing machine, white and dormant and waiting to be emptied, Beth-Ann remembered.

She felt suddenly conspicuous, as if it was she who was hiding and not Dimitri; as if behind the washing machine was a normal place to dwell and she was strange for walking around in large and open spaces. She listened intently. No breathing.

Beth-Ann placed her hands firmly on top of the washing

machine. She pressed her toes against the floor. As her body rose, so did her heart rate; she was prepared to be startled, but still felt scared. She wondered if it was better to know or better to be snuck up on. She felt a wave of pleasant sickness crawl across her abdomen as she strained to look over the dial panel of the machine.

But there was nothing behind it. No blue Dimitri eyes, bright like a Husky's; no dark and straight-combed Dimitri hair, black like a crow's feathers. Only dust and lint and hoses and one black sock. Beth-Ann couldn't help but feel disappointed.

After deciding the sock was definitely not hers, she began to hurry. She opened the washer and grabbed a large clump of cold, wet clothes. Holding them against her chest with one hand, she bent and opened the dryer door with the other.

"OOGAH-OOGAH-OOGAH!"

Beth-Ann screamed a short, high-pitched yelp. She dropped her clean clothes on the floor. Her heart beat in her throat, and she could feel the pulse in her temples without touching them. Maybe getting snuck up on *was* better.

Dimitri was curled up inside the dryer like a folded sock, lying in a ball with his arms wrapped around his bent knees. His body filled the entire drum. He turned his head a little to the side, and through the mixed-up mess of arms and legs and hands and feet, his eyes met Beth-Ann's. "Oogah?" he said quietly, sweetly, as if asking if she was okay.

"That wasn't nice," Beth-Ann scolded, making the best angry face she could.

"Sorry."

"Come on. Get out of there. I want to do my drying."

Dimitri shifted his body around in the dryer. His head popped out of the opening, and he pushed the rest of himself out, falling gently to the floor on his back. He blinked in the light.

Beth-Ann immediately began throwing her wet clothes into the dryer. Damp shirts and soggy pants whipped by Dimitri's nose and chin. He kept an eye open for bras and underwear.

"You're in my way. Move it!"

Dimitri stood up and stretched his limbs. He said, "Here, let me help you."

Beth-Ann stared at him angrily, her brown eyes piercing him. She ran her fingers violently through her long brown hair and held a tuft of bangs aloft. Her furrowed brow obscured the freckles on her forehead. Her frowning lips looked dry. "Just get out of here," she spat. "Get away from me. Asshole."

Dimitri shrugged his shoulders. "Sorry." He turned and drifted off.

Beth-Ann pretended not to watch him traipsing toward the parking garage.

Beth-Ann lay on her back on the couch, her head propped up against two cushions. She couldn't concentrate on her remote. She stuffed her mouth with vinegar chips, a slow but constant procession, and allowed the commercials and boring parts of the television programs to play out on her screen. She wondered if she and Dimitri were the only tenants in their building home tonight; home, instead of out at a club or a movie, like normal people on Saturday nights. She told herself it was still early, that she didn't have to stay in all night. She remembered telling herself the same thing the weekend before.

She pictured Dimitri in the dryer and tried to recreate the split-second of terror she'd felt in the laundry room. It wasn't the same as the real thing.

Her chip bag was empty. She took a big sip of Pepsi. She brushed the chip crumbs off the front of her shirt with the tips of her fingers. She continued brushing her chest even after all the crumbs were gone.

Beth-Ann left the couch after staring at the news for ten inattentive minutes. She stepped quietly out of the elevator into the basement and saw her laundry basket filled with clothes, dry and folded. Her throat felt parched.

She reached into the basket and took one of her t-shirts from the top of the pile. It wasn't folded exactly the way she liked. "But not a bad job for a guy," she thought. She pictured Dimitri folding her clothes, putting his hands all over them. A chill crawled down the back of her neck and spread to her shoulders. She shuddered and her teeth chattered for a second.

Beth-Ann reached slowly for the dryer door and yanked it open. Empty. Of course, she thought, it was still way too hot to go inside. "Hello?" she sang. "Where are you?" Beth-Ann crept past the washing machine and tip-toed around the side. Steadying herself for a fright, she peeked behind it, but saw nothing. Just dust and lint and the one lone sock like before. "Dimitri?" she called. The laundry room was appallingly still, hideously quiet.

Beth-Ann placed her left foot between the back of the washing machine and the wall. She wedged her left hip into the space. The rest of her body followed. She had to duck under the hoses, and allowed her back to slide down against the wall until she was crouching. Her drawn-up thighs pushed hard against her stomach and chest. She wrapped her arms around her bent knees and clasped her hands together. She began to breathe loudly. She felt dust in the back of her throat. And she waited.

Ramadan

She works the flour and water with sprinkles of salt. Into the middle goes an egg. She sinks her fingers, rolling the palm of her hand to this side and that. Shoulders push down from the hip, lips creasing in small lines the harder she pushes and the faster she rolls and the deeper she rocks.

When that is done she pulls it into lumps. Rolling, flattening, and dividing into smaller lumps. Some knotted, some pressed into rows, some dunked in sugar and nuts, some thrown over the balcony to the dogs.

No time to watch the oven, no time to check the clock, but the television is on. Her back to the screen, she is rolling and pushing and heaving the dough as the dogs groan go, go, go. She doesn't count the cookies, but they fill the bowls, and she covers them with damp towels, damp shirts, damp shorts, damp socks. Draining the teacup, she lingers on the sugar, sucking the tiny leaves between her teeth.

Now and then her eyes are wide open. She passes the television on the way to the balcony. Leans over to shake the rope to see that the basket is empty. Inside, the television's dim light reflects blue on her pallid skin, but her ears stay outside, and she hears the clip of donkey feet and the scrape of wooden wheels and the cries of the man who will fill up her basket. She runs back out and waves. She lowers him a cookie. He loads tomatoes to squeeze, lettuce to break, onions to slice, and potatoes to wipe the dirt from. She will pay him tomorrow.

The rope is old but it never breaks. She pulls it up and puts the food in the sink, turning on the cold water, which in the summer is always hot.

The television is close by. Close to her back, to the bowls of cookies, close and closer. There are fat and happy cows dancing with their udders in the air. She listens to the song and opens the fridge, letting the cool cold air blow her back out to the balcony. A boy on the crossways crisscross street stops when he hears her voice, "*Ya Walid!*" She lowers him money. He skips in a zigzag to the little store on the corner, walks in a zigzag back to the balcony, puts a bottle of milk into the basket. She gives him a cookie. He asks for another.

Three dozen cookies come out of the oven all at once, and three dozen more slide right back in. She sits on the floor, her feet under her legs, the weight of her belly and her breasts and her shoulders and her head rolling and rocking into the dough. She pushes the dough ball into three dozen more.

The music on the television makes her belly shiver, and sometimes she twirls a hand in the air to dance with the flies. The voice of the woman brings tears to her eyes. The voice, that voice, meeting the night. The words infuse her head leaving stains like leaves in hot water. *Aqbal il-leil*. The sun glares off the screen, the afternoon wind pushing the curtains into clouds that billow against her back. Her doughy arms waft into the air, throwing shadows of flour smudges onto her cheeks. The dogs have come again beneath the balcony. The street begins to squeal with children in their dusty green uniforms. She throws some cookies out over the balcony and heaves her body back to work.

She doesn't have an iron, and her clothes keep wrinkling. Under her arms and down her back and at the folds of her belly the fabric meets and gathers into streaks of the day's work. She washes her dress. From under the beds and behind the couch and in the corners she hunts for all the dirty clothes. She scrubs, pounds, and bends over them like they were cookies. She pulls and tears at them as if she was to tear them apart. At the edge of the tub she kneels. Wet legs, wet arms, wet shoulders, wet red fingers deep in the creases of fabric, lost in the humid dirt, probing through traces of flour and cookies and dogs and spit. So slowly she straightens her back and goes to the balcony. The street is coming and going and tossing itself up to her feet in handfuls of dust and dried leaves. She shakes out the wet clothes, her hands gripping the corners of each piece, shaking, flapping them into her legs, beating mountains into flat plains.

Shirts and pants and dresses hang over the line shaking, shaking, shrinking in the wind.

The afternoon is almost over. She falls to her knees again and again, lips moving silently, eyelids fluttering, fingers shaking. In her prayers she sings those words. That voice, that voice, that voice. She rides up to the night on a donkey's back tasting the lips of the lover. This is how she always prays. She tells no-one.

Her husband comes home, and he eats her food; her children come home, and they eat her food. The fasting has imploded with the sound of the gun, with the music on the television, with the banging of fists in rice. The hunger, the hunger. She hears that voice again. She rides a donkey's back. The television is on, and she sits in front of it, but first she washes dishes. Her husband yells out the jokes she has missed, and her children yell out to each other.

She dries her hands on her lap, smokes a cigarette, eyes dropping, mouth relaxing. The television is telling stories that she believes are true, so she falls asleep and dreams. Later, her children are tired and her husband is tired, so she wakes up to fix the beds. She eats more food. The food is cold to her dark lips. She takes in the dry grey clothes and folds them into piles like stale bread and lets her eyes droop and mouth relax and head fall on a pile of sheets, and there she sleeps.

Bonk Fish

Now people say the blues is about persecution and loss and the experience of being black and powerless in America.

And this is true, and it makes me wonder how I can even connect to the blues. I am a white man, and when I grew up I always had as many sandwiches as I liked.

And there is no way that you can call me a professional emotional person. I leave that to fully qualified people such as my wife's cousin Alannah who just shot her fourth husband. She didn't shoot all four ... It just happened that her fourth husband Leon was the one she shot.

She had said to him, "You don't love me!!!" and he had made the mistake of not looking up from the baseball game or whatever it was he was watching, and the next thing you know she had fired through the back of the Lazy Boy and the bullet had lodged itself deep in the muscle of his hindquarters.

Now some people consider this to be a humorous injury, and, when compared with other places a bullet can go, maybe it is. But as Leon rose injured and bleeding from his chair he did not see the funny side. She did not look the least bit contrite, nor had she put the gun down, and he often felt later that the only reason she didn't shoot him again was because of how badly he was bleeding onto her rug.

To her credit she did not worry solely about the rug, and, when she found that she could not staunch the flow, she even began to panic, pleading with the 911 operator to send an ambulance. It was the operator's idea to include a side order of two or three police cars, and this despite the fact that – as she continued to tell all and sundry – the whole thing was a silly accident.

As the two ambulance men tried to float Leon's enormous bulk down from the second floor without smacking his punctured posterior on the stairs, the air was punctuated by the sound of him yelling.

"Lock the bitch up she's dangerous O God she shot me I'm gonna die!!! Don't turn your back on her!"

Leon did not mean this, of course.

Well, he did mean it. At the time he meant it. But, however deep his immediate outrage and shock, he still understood that she had shot him out of love. But he wanted to make it perfectly clear to her – clear beyond the shadow of any possible misunderstanding – that he would not ever again tolerate any expression of her feelings that involved shooting him.

Because, far from being contrite, Alannah was experiencing no end of fulfillment. There were so many options. Should she feel deeply guilty for plugging and nearly killing the man she loved, who at this very moment was bleeding himself white at the General Hospital? Or should she be more upset at the utter callousness to her feelings that he had shown by allowing her to reach such a peak of despair and misery that she had felt compelled to plug him for his own good?

Now I have never felt lack of love so deeply that I have desired to plug the one I loved. And I suppose in many people's books this makes me less of an artist.

"How can you be an artist?" they say. "You just don't feel deeply enough." At which time I point out that my wife's cousin Alannah seems to feel plenty, but that doesn't make her any Michelangelo either.

But I do feel the blues, and there is no doubt about this. Because here is the mixture we are talking about, and it is a very potent mixture because it feeds three very separate desires in us:

the desire for novelty, the desire for control, and the desire for emotional release.

Now in your desire for control there is great comfort. Because it makes us feel that

- in this incomprehensibly vast universe, where neutron stars are stripped of electrons and crushed into a matter soup so dense that a teaspoon would weigh as much as the planet Earth–
- in this place where I cannot say why I was born or when I will die–
- in this seemingly random panorama of violence and oppression–
- in my total inability to predict or control anything, even my mood–

one thing is certain, and that is that somewhere in the blues Muddy Waters will reach for that fifth chord in the key of G and then return me to where I belong.

I do not know exactly how he will get there, but I know that he will get there. And in that I am rocked by the lullaby of sure knowledge of his escape from – and return to – the root chord of the key in which he plays.

Now this is a very powerful thing, and you can tell how powerful by asking anyone with children. My oldest child Michael is two and a half now, and for him the universe can be a very unpredictable place. Sometimes it will become completely skewed, and he will not know whether he is asleep or awake or where his parents are or what's happening and why. And these are all very terrifying things, and add to them the unpredictable moods of his parents – well his father anyway – and you have a formula where the predictable becomes very desirable.

In response to this onslaught of unpredictability, we do things with a certain sense of order and ritual. For instance, ever since his sister was born I take him to bed at night, and invariably he kisses his mother, and then I carry him down the hall, and we stop just inside the door of his room – where the mobile of multicoloured wooden tropical fish hangs – and we take our foreheads, and we bonk these fish until they rattle and fly in all directions, and we salute each other by turning our foreheads as if to bonk each other, and we finish with our two foreheads just touching, his right temple against my left as we walk towards the window.

At the window we say goodnight to the unseen birds who inhabit the alley, sleeping hidden between crumbling bricks, on balconies and under the broken flashing of the rooftops. And on clear nights we say goodnight to the moving searchlight on Place Ville Marie. And to the shiny, lit-up roof of the Place de la Cathédrale beside it.

And these are things we both know will happen, and they rock us in the same way a good blues does. And just like this sense of ritual is always alive, blues songs are capable of intense transformations from one occasion to the next, even from one verse to the next.

The blues just didn't crawl up out of nowhere ...

And the same holds true of our actions. You may say to yourselves, "Why do these people bonk the fish with their foreheads?" The answer is that, well, in the beginning we didn't bonk the fish at all.

We started off by saying goodnight to the missing birds, and then one night Michael added the fish.

He was also the first to stir the fish with his hand, one night as we walked by them. And he found that stirring the fish was good, and after this he stirred those fish for a good many nights.

And later, as he grew conscious of the power he had over the fish, he became more violent with them and favoured a wild swatting motion that sent them flying in such high orbit that the nylon strings from which they were suspended became hopelessly entangled.

At this point that I ventured the opinion that perhaps he should not whack the fish with such violence. But it is a truth of existence that having once demolished the fish with a single blow, it becomes difficult to withdraw to the more docile stirring of the fish without a feeling of loss.

And it was in this context that Michael came up with the brilliant alternative of bonking the fish with his forehead, which has all the thrill of the fish rocking inches from his eyes, and at the same time is much less likely to tangle the strings supporting them.

And I, of course – in some transformation of the way we learn from our elders – copied this from him, and now I too bonk the fish.

And lately other things are changing as well. For instance, on those nights when the moon is visible from our window, we include this moon in our nightly aloha to the universe and comment on its size and shape and its relationship to the clouds in the sky.

The moon is a transient. It doesn't appear in all the shows, but when it does make an entrance it tends to steal centre stage. And like the broken-hearted wailing of Little Walter on those early Muddy Waters tunes – wild, distorted, human – it is very hard to take your attention away from it once you've experienced it.

Little Walter is not the complete orchestra, nor did he ever achieve even top billing when Muddy was around, but once you hear Little Walter play, the rest of the tune – which seemed quite adequate and even beautiful before the harp came in – cannot continue by itself and wraps up as quickly as possible.

My existence was perfectly adequate, too, before Michael and his sister were born. But I confess it never occurred to me to bonk fish with my forehead. And it seems hard to believe that I considered the little I did have then to be enough to call it my life.

FlipFlop

She loves them. She can't remember who gave them to her, thinks maybe it was a neighbour. She even likes the name: *flip-flops*. These are bright coral, with a large pink and yellow plastic flower on top of each foot, where the straps cross. Very elegant. The part underneath her feet is white, and she can just glimpse bits of it when she wiggles her toes. She has been wearing them constantly for days now (how long has it been? she can't tell, she can't keep all the days apart to count them), and when she can be persuaded to take them off for a few minutes, to clean her feet properly, there is a pale footprint in each sandal. She watches her swinging, dusty feet admiringly.

> *one two buckle my shoe*
> *three four shut the door*
> *five six pick up sticks*
> *seven eight lay them straight*
> *nine ten—*

They've been driving forever, and, when she looks up from her feet, she sees that they are nearly at the top of the mountain now, driving along a narrow, twisting road with a sheer drop to the turquoise glare of the sea hundreds of feet below. They stop, briefly, to let a couple of knobby goats cross the road. The animals start nibbling on some olive-coloured shrubs, turning their triangular little heads and slanty eyes when the car starts up again.

One of the women in front asks the girl if she is thirsty. She does not give any sign that she has heard and continues to watch the glittering water. The waves burn and clatter under the strong sun, so that it is difficult to stare down for too long. She closes her eyes briefly and watches the red-black flowers explode against her eyelids. When she was hiding in the bougainvillea this morning, she heard one of them say that anyway she wasn't like a proper child, too quiet, always looking at you, and you could never tell what she was thinking.

Her aunt sighs now and asks the little boy if he'd like some juice, tells him to offer some to his cousin as well. She feels him slide the bottle of pineapple juice towards her, across the warm, cracked vinyl of the back seat. Without looking, she reaches for the bottle and takes a sip, returns it. She likes him actually. He doesn't try to get her to speak, and they play silent, intense games involving hieroglyphic messages left for each other on scraps of paper and hours of hiding in dark, cramped spaces. She likes his skin, which looks like chocolate, though it only tasted of seawater and dust when she licked his shoulder.

When the older girl who lived upstairs pointed out once that she and her mother were different colours, they nearly got into a fight. She finally brought the neighbour over triumphantly to show how the skin on the inside of her arm (where it wasn't dark from the sun) was the same colour as her mother's. They'd spent the rest of the afternoon being singing stars, jumping on the bed with towels on their heads and waving around hairbrush microphones. She wore the yellow towel as long blond hair and made the other girl take the faded green.

Snowy streets, her red boots, the scratched yellow kitchen table, the orange and brown living room carpet. Chocolate milk and the tattered scrap of flannel from her baby blanket she keeps under her pillow. She realizes she doesn't know the name of the place where her mother is now. Still staring fixedly out the window, she pinches the little boy hard. She does not react to his surprised yelp. She frowns sternly and whispers the word snow. The name of the place where she lives is lost. She does not answer when he asks her what snow is.

She thinks perhaps this is her fault, being here, because, when her father came to pick her up at nursery school one afternoon, she panicked and went with him, though she was sure this wasn't meant to happen. Trotting to keep up with her father's rapid, scissor stride, she clutched the bag with her precious sandals – it was lucky she'd brought them to show the teacher that morning. When they got to the airport, he phoned her mother, muttering quietly into the receiver, ignoring her insistent tugs on his pant leg. She sobbed finally that she wanted to talk to mommy too, to tell her to come get her, but her father did not seem to hear; he hung up quickly. Before they got on the plane he bought her some french fries, which she carefully did not eat. She decorated them with small strips of ketchup from foil packets until her father took the plate away. They sat next to a glass wall until it was time to leave, and on the other side planes were sucked up and away into the blue.

She hasn't spoken to anyone since, except for a few whispered words to her cousin. Still staring out the window, she pinches him again. The aunts are talking about her in the front seat, as if she can't understand. Well, actually, sometimes she can't, because they switch back and forth to a kind of singing language whose slithery rhythms remind her of the noisy sea. The softer one with plump hands like grapes sighs again and says he should really bring her back to her mother, it's not right. The pointy one with skin like ashes dropped in coffee says something about *white people* and *unnatural* and *not family,* spitting out the words like little stones, like blown grit, so that they prickle in the girl's eyes. Nobody has seen her father in days. The aunts' voices grow fine edges around his name, the softer one using words like *disgrace,* which she pronounces richly and rolling like the name of a poisonous fruit, while the pointy one reprimands – he was always the naughty boy, this place had always been too small for him, and what harm was there in going to the casino on the next island. Eventually, they lapse into tight silence.

The girl swings her feet more quickly and feels her heart galloping along: flip-flop, flip-flop. It leaps and shivers in her chest. The boy has fallen asleep in a tangle of spidery arms and legs, curled up in the other corner. Her legs stick to the seat as she tries to move closer to the window. The hot wind billows and rushes against her face like a large hand covering her nose and mouth, so that she has to turn her head slightly to get enough air. It smells like dust and all the prickly dense green things that twist out of the sandy dirt here. Her cousin showed her how they had a secret inside – you could tear them open and they'd be full of clear slimy juice that soothed your skin if you had a scratch or a burn. She wanted to know what happened if you drank it, but her throat felt creaky from all the words stopped up.

She watches the shiny black road being swallowed up by the car, which spits it out again behind them. She thinks of a story someone read to her a long time ago, about a small girl and her brother who lose their parents somewhere in the snow and they have to look for them in the woods and they leave a trail of bread crumbs so they can find their way back to the candy house. There were pictures too, and a witch, but now it has all become tangled up with other stories and she just remembers the trail of crumbs clearly.

Flip-flop, flip-flop, goes her galloping heart, clattering across red fields on its little rubber hooves. She reaches down and pulls off one of her sandals. She holds it in her hand for a moment, then throws it out the window. She turns to watch it land on the hot tar behind them, rapidly shrinking as they fly on. Quite soon it disappears behind a curve in the road.

How I Met Cousin Biz

I was only thirteen when Biz moved to Thunder Hill. His family drove over for Mom's fish chowder. I made some chocolate-chip cookies for dessert, and Dad had gone into town to get beer.

"Here they come!" I shouted up the back stairs to Mom. A green Volvo bounced down the lane.

Mom came running down the stairs. She had gotten all dressed up to greet her half-brother, Arthur, his wife, Frances, and their two children. She was even wearing a long skirt over Dad's hunting socks. I could tell she was nervous because she practically shouted at me to wipe the crumbs off the table. I told her she should take a deep breath because it was just toast crumbs. As far as I'm concerned a few crumbs on the table look pretty normal.

We went out to meet them. Arthur was tall and pale. Kayla told me she was eight and then kept blinking her eyes. Frances wore a long skirt too. With thin strapped sandals. Not the kind you see old hippies wearing. But the thing I noticed the most was her nose. Looking like it had been pinched too often. She went right up to my mother and grasped both her hands. I wondered why she was laughing so much. But then again, so was Mom, in a *I don't know why we're laughing but I'll be a good sport about it* way.

"I'm so happy to meet you, finally," Frances said, grinning at my mother, who, I could tell, was trying not to be so rude as to look right around this woman so she might get a glimpse of Arthur.

Arthur, like I said, is Mom's half-brother. She has only met him once, and that was at Grandpa Kidd's funeral. Mom and

Arthur hardly knew what to say to each other then, and it didn't look like that was going to change much today, because after shaking her hand he stared at our chickens like it was the first time he'd ever seen them. It was summer, and I thought the yard looked pretty. I'd mown the lawn around the apple trees the day before, and now the evening sun made everything look golden green.

"Come on in," Mom said, "the chowder's just about ready."

We all turned to look at the car, since it was obvious that someone was still sitting in it. Frances, who I guessed was my half-aunt, kept saying that "Byron" was still adjusting to the country and that she was sure he would be in by dessert time. Except he would not be allowed any. She kept going out there to the car, and from the back door window I could see she was real mad at him because her face got all red as she banged on the window of the car. He had locked all the doors and was sitting in the back seat with his arms folded. Then half-aunt Frances (I wondered if I was supposed to call her that) came back in the house looking pretty flushed, but laughing louder and louder each time she came through the door.

"He can be very stubborn, our Byron," Frances said.

"A big brat," said Kayla.

"Don't worry about it," my mother told her, "sometimes it's better just to leave them alone."

"Not when it comes to rudeness," said half-aunt Frances, her mouth settling into a frown. "There are two things in this world I won't tolerate, and rudeness is one of them."

I thought my mother might ask her what the other thing was, but instead she said, "Give him time, he's probably just shy."

"Byron?" Frances laughed, "He's not shy at all, is he, Kayla?"

"No, ho, not shy. Like he tells everybody he meets that his real name is Biz instead of Byron."

"And is it?" my mother said.

"Is it what?" Frances said, sounding confused.

"Is his real name Biz?" I said, slowly.

"Of course not!" Frances and Kayla said, practically at the same time. Then Frances turned to Arthur. "Arthur? Would you say that our Byron was shy?"

"Sorry. What was that?" All this time, Arthur had been talking to Dad, who was loading beer into the bottom of the fridge. "I was talking to Tom about dogs. Remember? You said we should look into dog breeding?"

"Oh yes, Tom, I heard you used to breed collies. We were thinking we'd like to get involved in some sort of small business venture, like truck farming, or ostrich ranching, right Arthur? We want something for Arthur to do besides teaching at the University. Something to make him feel he lives in the country."

Both my Mom and Dad stared at Frances. My Dad joked, "Well, there's always pig farming."

"I have heard that pigs are very intelligent," Frances said seriously. "But don't they smell?"

Dad said, "They're actually very clean animals."

"You know? I've heard that too."

I could see Mom give Dad a little sideways kick in the shin, but he kept going with it anyway.

"You see, the beauty of pigs is that you don't need a lot of land since they're not big grazers like cattle. You just need a barn."

"We have a barn!"

"Don't listen to him," Mom said. "You wouldn't want pigs. They haven't made money in years and don't believe for a second that they don't stink."

"Oh," said Frances. She and Arthur stared at my Dad who grinned and said, "Anyone want a beer?"

"We used to show our dogs," I said, jumping off the stool we keep by the stove. "Look here at this album."

I showed them the photos of Witch, our blue merle, who once

won "Best in Show" for the whole province, and Prince, who won "Best in Class" three years in a row. Frances seemed very interested to know about dog shows, so I went on to tell her that Mom and Dad used to show a lot and that each of our pups used to be worth about four hundred dollars each.

Mom called us into the dining room. Then she ladled out the fish chowder and put the hot rolls in a basket.

"This is delicious," said Frances, "What kind of fish is it?"

"Flounder."

"Freshly caught, no doubt."

"Fresh out of the freezer."

"It's good," said Arthur.

"Yes it's yummy," said Kayla, who was filling up on rolls.

"So, tell me, why didn't you stay in the dog business?" Frances wanted to know.

"It got to be too much," Mom said. "With both of us working. I couldn't keep up."

Dad said," You didn't want to keep up."

Mom got up, "I'll go get napkins."

"So all we got left is smelly old Susie," I said – and then felt bad when everyone laughed because Susie lifted her head off the floor at the sound of her name.

"I'd like to have Weimaraners," Frances said. "They are the most beautiful dogs. Have you ever seen them? Their coats feel like velvet, and they're such a beautiful bluish-grey."

"Not hardy enough for me," Mom said, and I felt proud because my mother knows all about dogs and what you can expect from them. She used to show them too. But mostly for the people who bought our pups. Here they were, our pups, we handled them, and the people who bought them got all the credit. As if they had anything to do with the bloodlines or the training. You think it's that easy to get a dog to stand at attention while strangers first open their jaws to inspect their bite and then reach down to check if they have both balls?

"Can I get you more chowder, Arthur?" Mom said, coming in with the pot again.

"Oh, no thanks, I think I'll save some room for the next course."

My Mom stopped mid-step and said to Frances, "When I said we were having fish chowder, I meant fish chowder was all we were having."

"Oh dear, I am so sorry!" Frances said with this horrified voice, "This is my fault entirely, I told Arthur only that we were coming for supper."

"No, I am the one who is sorry," Arthur said. He was about as red as the chowder pot. "For my presumptuousness."

They all started laughing then, like someone had said something funny. But then that stopped and the only sound in the room came from the floor where Susie was licking her privates. I gave her a little kick to get her to stop.

Then Mom told me to take Susie out and show cousin Kayla the new kittens out in the shed.

"But don't touch the kittens," Frances said, and I heard her tell my mother, "She has allergies."

So we went out to the yard past the Volvo in which this boy named Byron stared straight ahead. When we walked in front of the car he turned his head the other way. I kept walking around and around the car, which meant he had to keep moving his head to avoid me. I must have gone around at least five times before he finally gave me the finger. I gave it back to him, and then I took Kayla to see the kittens.

The Sound of Leaving

Bonnie was six when her mother left her father. She didn't know at the time that her father was the one who had been left. Instead she imagined wrongs she had done, terrible things she must have said to hurt her mother's feelings. Years later she would often replay her mother's leaving all over again, see those slim legs walking away, the seams of nylons running right down into the thick heels of her high, black shoes. Bonnie saw her mother get into the yellow taxicab with the black and white squares painted like a checkerboard on the side, heard her own young voice scream "Mommy! Mommy!" as the car drove away. They did not see each other again until Bonnie had her first child, Matthew.

Matthew was just a few months old when she got the phone call.

"Hello?"

"Bonnie?" asked the voice at the other end.

"Yes, this is Bonnie."

"Bonnie, it's Lorna. Mum."

Bonnie hung up the phone.

Six months later it was the doorbell that rang. Looking back afterward, Bonnie remembered the time of day and what she had been wearing. It wasn't quite nine a.m.; she had just put Matthew down for his morning nap and was about to have her coffee. She walked towards the front door while pulling her green housecoat tighter around her, using the fingers on her free hand to comb through her long, brown hair. There had been a patch of sunlight on the rug in the front entrance. Bonnie would always see her hand reaching for the doorknob, twisting it to the right, pulling the door in towards herself until she was staring at the sad, solemn face of her mother.

She didn't need the old photos to recognize her, nor the strong resemblance between them. It was enough to see the woman who stood there, and for over a minute Bonnie looked at her without saying a word, not even hello. Then Lorna had slowly leaned forward, reached out her hand, and touched her daughter's left cheek, lightly stroking a line with her fingertips to the edge of the younger woman's mouth. Bonnie had stepped back then, and her mother followed her with a step forward.

"I wanted to–" "What are you–" they said at the same time. Both paused, waiting.

"What are you doing here?" asked Bonnie, this time louder.

"I wanted to see you. Your child."

"How do you know about Matthew?"

"Matthew. A boy." Her mother's voice sounded like a caress. "I thought you knew."

"I've seen you both from afar, but I never got close enough to see him. It … it's a beautiful name – thank you."

"I didn't choose his name because of you," replied Bonnie.

"But my father?"

"My husband is partial to the name. It has nothing to do with you."

"Oh," said Lorna.

There was a long silence then, the quiet so deep it was as if neither of them had enough air to breathe. Bonnie looked at her mother. She must have been nearly fifty. She was wearing a light purple skirt, a white, long-sleeved shirt and hoop earrings. Bonnie remembered being outraged at this last detail, *hoop earrings!* she had thought. *The audacity!* As if the woman was young and pretty. As if she could have fun.

"Bonnie, may I come in?"

"I don't know, Matthew's sleeping …"

"I won't wake him. I'd like to sit with you, talk maybe."

"I can't imagine what you'd have to say."

"May I?" her mother had persisted. Bonnie lingered then, staring into Lorna's eyes and willing the tears forming there to fall. But Lorna steeled herself and did not cry.

Bonnie said, "OK. I guess you may as well come in. Since you're here."

"Thank you."

Bonnie shut the door as her mother entered the house, then turned and led her into the kitchen. The white linoleum had not been swept that day, and the morning's crumbs speckled the bright floor.

"I haven't dressed yet," said the young woman automatically. "I was about to have my coffee."

"That's alright."

"Would you like some? Coffee?"

"No, thank you. Mind if I smoke?"

"Until Matthew wakes up; I'll just open a window."

"I don't have to."

"No, that's OK. William sometimes has one in the evening."

"Your husband?" Lorna asked as she lit her cigarette.

"Yes." Bonnie sat down on the yellow wooden chair, pouring coffee into the cup that had been standing empty. "He's at work."

"What does he do?" asked Lorna.

"He sells insurance."

"Oh."

This was often the flat response Bonnie got when she told people what her husband did, as if they would have been more pleased if he'd been a race car driver or a spy.

"He's a good man," she said quickly. "He stays home, with me and Matthew."

"Yes." Lorna's voice was quiet but self-assured. "Bonnie," she began, "I ... I'm sorry I didn't stay in touch. You might not believe this, but it was for the best."

"I'm sure," said her daughter drily.

"No, really. I was extremely unhappy. I had made a mess of my life – I would have made a mess of yours."

"You had a good go at it though, didn't you?" Bonnie shot back.

"I drank – I used the switch on you. Do you remember?" asked Lorna.

Bonnie pushed herself away from the table; the legs of her chair made a dry sound as they scraped across the linoleum. "Let me get an ashtray," she said. "That ash is getting awfully long."

"Bonnie," continued her mother, her voice cracking and rising, "I'm sorry."

"Yes, well, isn't everybody."

"Everybody?" queried Lorna. "Even you? What are you sorry for?"

Bonnie took her seat, placing the ashtray between her and her mother on the table. "I'm sorry I let you in," she answered.

"When?" asked Lorna softly.

"What do you mean, when? This morning, in the door!"

"Right." Lorna took a long drag on her cigarette, inhaling deeply.

Bonnie could see a yellow stain between the fingers with which her mother held the cigarette.

"Can I see Matthew?" asked Lorna.

"He's asleep."

"I won't wake him. I just want to look," said her mother.

"It's dim in there. You won't see much."

"That's alright," Lorna said as she stubbed out the cigarette. She stood up.

"This way," said Bonnie, and she stood and led Lorna out of the kitchen, walking in the direction they had come in. They walked towards the front of the house, then Bonnie opened the front door and indicated that her mother should leave.

"Bonnie, please, I ..." Lorna stammered.

"I think you've been here long enough. Please don't come back." Bonnie looked outdoors while saying this, saw the large oak tree across the yard shimmer in the sunlight, its foliage bright and green. She watched her mother's retreating back as the woman slowly passed her and went out the door. As Lorna descended the three concrete steps, Bonnie expected to hear the efficient click of heels. Instead she barely heard a beat. She looked down. *Sandals,* she thought.

She closed the door firmly and went to the small room off the kitchen where her son slept. She opened the door and walked quietly to his crib. He was sleeping peacefully, wearing a pale-blue jumper. As Bonnie stood there his eyes opened and he looked at her, unblinking.

She wiped the tears that ran down her face. "You look just like her," she said.

2000-2001

NEALE MCDEVITT

Honey-Tongued Hooker

Yesterday I passed a fourteen-year-old hooker by the Dunkin'
Donuts. Maybe fifteen. She had shoehorned her little-boy ass into
a pair of white tights that looked like they were peeled off a Barbie
doll. This baby slut was no Barbie doll, though. No fucking way.
Barbie has healthy pink skin and big blue eyes painted on an
unblemished face. This tramp was all glazed and bloodshot. Her
eyes hung heavy on her face.

But there was something happening back there behind the
thousand-cock stare. Thinking back to sunny times on the farm?
To schoolyard days playing Red Rover with her friends and being
teased by freckle-faced boys? Maybe. But I doubted it. I figured
she wasn't thinking much beyond getting a batch of forgetfulness
stuck in her arm or up her nose, or reeling in another two-legged
meal ticket. Talk about a daily grind.

"Wanna date, honey?" she asked in a little voice as I passed.
Honey? I hadn't been called that since I was a kid mugging around
at the motel pool run by one of my dad's friends. In summertime,
Dad would hold court on a lawn chair surrounded by his cronies,
the whole mob of them squeezed into Speedos, their flesh baked
hard like alligator hide. Just sizzling in the heat like happy iguanas
on Galapagos.

The women could have been movie mobsters' wives: dyed
blond hair stacked high and hard; sunglasses that got bigger each
year to hide crumbling eyes and once-sharp cheekbones; and
wired-up leopard bathing suits that creaked beneath the
prodigious weight of migratory bosoms. They'd sit there day after
day, summer after summer, faces turned in reverential sacrifice
toward the sun – the last of their Valentinos not yet lured away by

the transient mysteries of younger, firmer sirens. They coated themselves with oil, gobs of buttery lube. Basting like big-titted turkeys, complete with gobbler necks and heavy brown drumsticks.

The pool was a treat for me and my brother. We'd spend all day in the water, wrestling, swimming, holding our breaths, pissing in the shallow end – all that stuff that ices a kid's cake. When we got wrinkly and blue-lipped, we'd wrap ourselves in towels and worm ourselves in beside Dad.

The conversation between him and the boys was always the same: shit-funny slags being tossed around, and someone recounting the previous night's misadventures. They all used swear words like punctuation marks, and I revered them because they never changed the way they spoke when us kids skittered over. No rolling eyes or whispered pig Latin. I felt like I was privy to their secret, exciting world. I felt like an adult. Scrunched there beside my big, laughing dad and spun up in my terri-towel chrysalis, I was taught the invaluable lessons of humour and friendship and the community of men.

The wives sat in their gaggle on the outskirts of the sacred ring of lawn chairs chatting and scolding each other's brats. Every now and then they'd rattle their ice at me. "Honey," they'd yodel, "be a sweetheart and fetch me a rum and coke. Tell Sam to put it on Dutch's tab." Entranced by their conical breasts, I'd nod a dutiful yes and go water-bugging to the bartender. Sometimes I'd steal a sip on my way back. On those really sweet, sweaty days, when the sun hung up forever and the entire crew was there, I'd have a good little buzz going by the end of our stay. Hazy memories of warm summer days.

But this was no warm day at the pool, and this teenage ass merchant was about forty summers short of calling me honey. I stopped. She slipped out of the doorway and barged her tiny body into my open jacket. She repeated her offer, "Wanna date?" I instinctively shifted away from her, but she pressed her advantage. Her head was at my chest, and her cold, bloodless fingers brushed my hips. Those damaged blue eyes looked through me to the promise of a brief interlude from a winter's street corner.

She pushed up against me, pushed soft but persistent. They hardly moved at all, but her searching fingers felt like they were looking to trigger the latch to a secret door. Like she was standing in the claustrophobic antechamber just a wall away from spacious breathing rooms. Her liquid hands poured across my body's bumpy surface, seeping into each crevice and filling them with something more than just quiet desperation. I thought of a blind man lost in a cave or a swimmer trapped under lake ice, pressing up against the hard surface and squeezing into every hollow to claw at the bitter promises hiding in the cracks.

Except this girl wasn't looking for a way out, she wanted in. The good whores learn how to read a man in seconds so they can tailor their pitch appropriately and lay the right bait. Nice Guy, Shy First-Timer, Protector, Hound Dog, Mean Fucker; they have all our angles covered. This kid repulsed me in a real primordial way – like meat gone gag-sour in the summer – but something about her made me feel sorry, even guilty. And she sensed it, like a street dog smells fear, impaling herself – almost gratefully, imperceptibly – on each sliver of empathy that jabbed out from my eyes. And she wriggled – more grateful than ever – on their tiny hooks. She wanted more from me than seventy-five dollars.

Maybe the banks of her childhood had eroded and fallen into this malicious river way too fast. I glimpsed the crying child standing among the levee's ruins as dark adult water swirled unabated around her legs, obliterating carefree, happy times. Spilled ink on a page. No gradual transition to help callus her up. No protective cocoon in which to sprout grownup legs and eyes and strong arms to beat back the beasts and whoremasters. Suddenly there she was, the spent old hag in the little girl's shell, like those Russian dolls in reverse. The little one entombs the bigger one.

She pressed up against my chest, squeezing in on my heartbeat and lungs. I felt her cat mouth sucking up my breath. Her thin-boned hands burrowed like small sparrows in the snow, digging deep into the cold to scavenge some warmth from my sunny memories. I let her stand inside me for a spell. We both needed it.

Did I feel juiced for sex? Fuck. Don't ask. Did I take her up on her offer? Did I feel the bitter zing of melancholy prick itself through my skin, ease straight into my vein and mix with my filthy, lusty blood? All of the above, friend. Intoxicating. Terrifying. But you have to believe me, I really wanted to take her somewhere else. A swimming hole. A country brook. A lake. The endless possibilities of oceans. I wanted to wrestle around in shallow water and splash her face and rub off the trashy paint. Wipe her slate clean. Soak her with cannonballs and hot seats and the inconsequential beads of compassion. Instead, I took her to a motel. I thought maybe they had a pool.

Tundra

I opened my eyes again at seven. Seven … seven … seven. I was me and it was seven. Then the big tumour egg in my head busted and the black ink covered my brain and poured over my eyes, like blood after a head wound. It was seven and I had to go. Moran was still sleeping. What did he know? I love him and I can't stand him for the same reasons. "Get up we need to go," I say. He looks at me like he has no idea what I'm talking about and I want to hit him. My back hurts and I know that I have ink pockets around my eyes. " Moran, we have to go," I say again. "Come on, get dressed there's not time for breakfast, we'll get something on the way."

It's September and the seat of the truck is cold and hard. My back hurts and I blink painfully at the sun, which is pouring in, cruel and joyful. Moran climbs, happy to be in a place that he knows. His truck.

We stop at Dunkin' Donuts. We're near the bus station, so naturally a lot of people look lost though they are from right here.

Moran's omelet sandwich is stinking up the cab so badly I can't help but curse him for picking such a dumb thing to eat. I swear, he just doesn't think. That's what Mr. Tessier said when he fired him from the garage. He's a very nice guy, everyone here likes him, but he just doesn't think. Mr. Tessier told me and I told Moran. He shrugged and stood there. Waiting for me to do I don't know what … I worked at different jobs until this came up.

I borrowed money from Grandma and Grandpa to pay for this abortion. The just gave it to me. They were really quiet. Grandma disappeared into the bathroom for a while. I knew damn well that she was crying, but I don't know for what. Grandpa could only look at the floor when we heard her blowing her nose. I was going to wait until she came out but, *Christ*, how much did I have to put up with in return for this loan?

I was four months pregnant, or sixteen weeks. I wanted this baby. I wanted it more than I wanted Moran never to leave me. I wanted to prove to my screwed-up family that I could have my own family without their screwed-up crap. I wasn't going to mess with this kid. I didn't bother telling Mom. I only told Dad last Tuesday. This Tuesday, I'm on my way to the clinic. It's costing a lot because I'm right on the cusp, they say. One more week and it could not have been possible they say. We're already pushing it, they say.

The baby understood immediately and released me by pulling away, like it was the one who wanted to leave. When Dad asked, "How do you expect to support a child when you can't even support yourselves?" Moran looked across at me. The truth is, that that's when the baby understood. Like it was the one who answered the question. It knew alone. It said, all things considered, finally, it had to be going, but thanks.

"Moran, you can't park here, go around the back." My body felt like a block of ice, dense and numb. I tasted salt on my tongue. Moran didn't talk much usually, but today, he had even less to say. This was not fixing a fan belt. He didn't really know anything about it except that he had to be there for it. "Moran, you can't park here," I said again, irritated.

He stopped the motor, but left the key in the ignition. We were both pretty quiet. My brain was starting to get jammed up with all the stuff I'd been straining not to think about and I was afraid. I knew he was waiting for me to decide when we would leave the truck and go in. "Come on, let's go," I finally said.

We checked the address. The clinic looked like one of the other houses on the street. What had probably been some kid's bedroom was the waiting room. It was all white with those waiting room chairs, magazines, and a reception desk, but you still knew it had once been someone's bedroom. I guessed right that the operation would happen in the living room/dining room part of the house. A big table laid out. The doctor and the nurse standing by it like ghoulish hosts.

The doctor and the nurse don't really exist. Just zombies from a bad movie. A soap opera where I beg them to save the baby but they insist on saving me. Where I did everything to save the baby but family enemies infiltrated the operating room and "botched" the operation on purpose. And I lay there immobile as they paralyze me with their the special power in their glare.

I can only look deep into the white light above me and I am walking in the frozen tundra. At first the tundra seems like a really nothing, lonely place. I remember once I saw this show on TV about the plants that survive in the tundra. A lot of the times, you can't even tell they're there. They live under thick sheets of ice and snow until their day comes, until it gets warm. They freeze themselves for months at a time, so they can live again for a couple of weeks. You can't really say that they're asking for too much. But they probably wait for that time like hell, all bent under the snow.

In the tundra, it's hard to judge distances. You could start walking towards a spot and think it's really close but you could freeze to death trying to get there. Although everything looks the same all around, it isn't uncommon to be called by a certain direction. To make a sharp turn for no apparent reason. Even though wherever you turn looks exactly like where you turned away from.

In the tundra, they have these inuksuks, these piles of rocks that look like a guy pointing you in the right direction. There's never a sign that says where you're going to end up, just that there's something in that direction. Regardless, you're probably really glad when you come across one. Maybe it's because it means that, once, someone else stood here and knew something, anything. And even though they are long gone, they may even have died before they got anywhere, you can still feel their certainty on the stones. And for a moment, it *is* home.

They said, "Wait before you get up."

Moran looked worried and glad to see me. Something else too. I don't know what.

Exhausted, I pulled off my jeans and crawled under the blankets half-dressed. I called Grandma and Dad between my first sleep and my second sleep. All that day and all that night, I thought I heard the television on in the living room.

EARL MURPHY

Antoine's Dog

For Alex, Adrien, and Jessica

It was cold this last winter. Lots of snow. Unusual to have snow with cold. A winter not fit for a dog, as they say. Though some like the cold, I suppose. Not me. I used to. When you're young, you can stand anything. Now, with my weak heart, the snow's as likely to kill me as the cold. Last winter I thought I'd up and die, and nobody'd be the wiser. There I'd be, come spring, thawed around the edges, heart hard as stone, eyes like ice cubes staring at heaven knows what, teeth still chattering from that godawful cold.

The wind screeched night and day.

The cracks in the wall around the edges of the windows and doors are stuffed to bursting with bits of rag and paper. Still, in the high wind, the floor near the cracks was littered with drops of melted snow like dew in summer. The wind howled, whistled through the cracks, searched me out, then crawled down my back, along my spine, neck to tail end. No matter how much wood I put in that stove the chill spread to fill every ounce of me. That's how bad it was.

Antoine's my nearest neighbour, a mile, mile and a half away. Now that's fine with me – fine with Antoine too I'd imagine – but there are times when being so far away is downright unneighbourly. With the split wood running out, snow half-way up the door and that cold wind blowing, it would have been neighbourly for him to offer to help. Antoine's my age, but strong as an ox. Why, he can tend more traps than ten men like me put together. All the way up to the fork in the river and in deep snow besides.

And that wife of his, name's Lucie, she can sure cook up a storm. Friendly too. Why sometimes it seems she cooks them spare-rib dinners just for me.

Must've dug enough snow to fill my grave a hundred times over. Come spring I was alive but just barely kicking. Then it began to snow again, and it never let up. Not for three days.

The third night I heard a howling over the sound of the wind that set me to dreaming of banshees and bogeymen prowling the dark. Come morning it was clear. Quiet. So quiet it almost hurt. My mother, bless her soul, called it the silence of angels. They stand quietly, she said, their wings folded neatly behind them, waiting for some creature to die.

The barking began at noon under a strong sun. Never let up. Before dark I dug my way out. Snow piled higher than I've ever seen it. The sky was deep red behind the trees, the snow dark like the ocean. And somewhere out in the wood by the main road, that God-forsaken dog. Must've heard me, or smelled me. It started in to yip and squeal like it was trying to tell me something.

Figured it was one of Antoine's dogs. But they never wandered this far. Except for that husky, a mean bugger like his master. It killed two of Antoine's dogs last fall. Antoine chained it, then beat it half to death. Better off dead, if you ask me. And that chain. A heavy thing. Links the size of my fist.

Couldn't get that dog out of my head. That thing howling out there, waiting for me. Enough to drive a man mad.

That storm broke the winter's back. Water poured off the roof in torrents. I swear a good foot of snow melted that night. By morning I could see clear across the meadow to the trees. Couldn't see the dog. Heard it yipping and whining though. Then by ten, eleven that day it just stopped.

Times when I wondered if it wasn't all in my head. A man by himself. At my age. Can't say I'm not scared at times. Mostly it's what I can't see scares me. The wind. The forest buried in fog.

Noises when it's quiet.

Spring's when fear is real. Tending traps out by way of Chaudière and Morris Falls. It's low ground and wet. Everything moves up a notch. Streams become rivers. Rivers get real angry. The bears are hungry. The wolves are like mad dogs. Hell, I feel ornery myself, putting up with it all.

But last spring it was the dog had me spooked. Had me hearing things. Seemed worse once the barking stopped. One thing I learned in my life. You stay away from places when there's only silence. It's best to let things be.

A week setting traps, hauling and skinning, working my way around that patch of wood near the road. Never set foot there the whole time. That dog was there waiting. Sure as hell.

Nature has a way of working that's slow and hurried all at once. Mountains sit thousands of years without moving. Then a leaf appears out of nowhere. A man's curiosity is a lot like that leaf. A small bud, then a spurt of growth. A week's a long time in the bush. Time works on a man. Tells him there's an itch in his hide needs scratching.

One morning a stag entered the wood. Looking for bare spots to graze. I figured the coast was clear then for sure. Still, I took my time. Breakfast first. Then my rifle. Cleaned it and loaded it.

There was still lots of snow in there. That deer wouldn't have found much. Except maybe that chain. Its great links rusted. Almost the colour of blood. And the dog hanging from it about a foot from the melting snow.

I've killed a few animals in my day, but I've never seen eyes so scared. And cold. Cold as ice.

That dog could've broke free and strayed. Then tangled itself in the low branches. Then again maybe it didn't. Now, I may be wrong, but I figure Antoine had it all worked to happen by itself. Nice and slow. Chained the dog to that branch and let the melting snow do the rest.

I told Antoine I found his dog and could he come take it down. Didn't say anything else. He didn't ask where it was or how it died. Didn't have to. "Sure thing," he said with that grin on his face and that look in his eyes.

They say God'll forgive a man most anything. But not what he did to that dog. Still, there's got to be a reason. Most days I wonder what that reason is. And why in that wood just across from my place?

Well, one thing's for sure. I'd best stay away from Antoine's place for now. Let him and his woman be. Poor Lucie and her fine cooking might just have to wait awhile.

CELIA MCBRIDE

Backseat, Baby

Bullets hit the back windshield smack and bouncing off the glass.
Ducking low in the backseat little enough to not get hit. Back and
forth we drive this road between our home and the main road is
black and smoother quiet calm. With each crack a gravel bullet
with each crack the glass might break. Never breaks it never does
but sounds like bullets so it is.

Another visit here we go. Who this time? "Folks," Mom says.
Where this time? Can't read the sign the sign says, "Bridgetown."
Mom's visits are important she has to have her fun at least. Finally
night and crickets sing coming home we turn the car and hear
the bullets. Who's the shooters? Imagine boys in masks with guns
running through the corn. They're never seen thank Hank for
that.

Mom says, "Thank Hank, instead," to Billy when he says,
"Thank Christ," for something. "You mean Hank Williams?" Billy
asks. Mom says, "He's close enough to Jesus, right?" Billy's laughing
that feels good. Inside somewhere is a wonder. Inside is quiet no-
one sees.

"Time to go." Mom yanks the breakfast plate banging it upon
the counter. Yellow whites blur away and breakfast's over. "You
can finish later, honey." But later never comes. Another day another
visit. Going again we're seeing folks. While we're gone fried strips
of pig are getting cold. That's what Billy called the bacon. But
Billy's gone and so it is.

Mom grabs the coffee pot out from dripping pulls it fast it
almost breaks. "Christ!" she says and doesn't notice. Hank's gone,
too. She should say Hank she's the one who made it up. Creepy
Joe snorts a laugh like a pig but he's not fried he's just creepy.

Mom pours the darkness into her enormous mug splashing drips on her new dress.

"Let's go," she says and slams the radio turns it off and ends the song. "Sorry, Loretta," Mom says and means it, too. The screen door bangs we're gone again. Bullets hit and ducking low. Listening to the cracking comforts crouching down behind the seat. Seat is blue it matches skirt is dirty knees and scratched up skin. Stomach rumbles keep it quiet.

Is it safe to peek up slowly? Is it safe to look the shooters in the eye?

Creepy Joe is talking low Mom is driving nodding answers. No words make it back behind them only whispers wind and sun. Sounding staying hushed and watching dust come through the cracks in puffs. Rattle bump we hit the main road no more bullets here on in.

What a world streams by in colours. Textures moving fast and gone. Poles and wires shacks and rusting tractors dogs on chains in empty yards. Untouchable yet touching something still somewhere is where it goes. Way down deep in hearts and blood.

Mom is on the sofa sleeping. Radio playing way too loud. Mom's cigarette is dangling from her lips. Al is snoring laying 'cross her squishing in her thighs like cushions. Creepy Joe is gone for good.

"Mom, radio is loud." Blasting noises down the hall. "Go to bed." She's half asleep. "Radio is loud." Blaring voices hit the room. "Sorry, kid," she says and shifts. Leans and finds the button presses off and butts her smoke. "Close the curtains willya, baby?" Carpet strands between the toes. Drawing curtains 'cross the window. Darkness crickets fireflies. Out there are boys with gravel bullets. Out there are angels back windshield. Flat and made of glass protect us angels keep us from the wounds. Out there is different soon to find it. Out there is growing up and gone.

Al grunts and moans and leave the room it's late enough.

"You like Al, hon'?" Truth is better lying squirms inside the heart. Shrug a nod and go to bed. Mom mumbles quiet Al won't last they never do.

Mom cannot find her keys. Lost and looking disappeared. Suitcase sitting by the door. Dust on suitcase catches sun and buckles glinting rusty gold. Comes inside through the screen the tiny specks are smaller than the little squares. Billy's suitcase from before he's coming by to pick it up. We won't be here Mom is itching wants to go and visit now. Now is never soon enough. But the place is a mess and Billy's coming he will see it and she cares.

"Christ!" she says. Let her say it. Saying Hank is not the way she really feels. Mom finds the keys and slams the door we're in the car one more time. One more visit one more man. One day these legs will know the front seat one day these hands will hold the wheel. Just the same as Mom once sat here small and wondering. Growing happens. Lives turn into one another. We're the same she and me and sometimes know it's true inside.

Al is quiet fewer whispers floating back. But he's funny Mom is laughing that feels good. Listen to the bullets cracking smacking sound of clicking dust. Don't look back don't want to see the boys aren't real don't want to know they don't exist. Growing older brings the truth. The bullets spit up from the tires. Sometimes knowing ruins things. Billy comes and gets his suitcase it is gone when we get back.

Driving sleepy. Visits places names and welcome. Population signs and laughter parties pretty folks and card games drinks. Cheezies chips and chocolate bars. Cigarettes glow and singers crying on the radio. Late night high times headlights home. Morning dew and waking slow. Whizzing speeds and farmers faces no-one ever sees. No-one sees the one small tear it squeezes shut and no-one noticed. All the world is waiting out there all the dust and all alone. In time the dust will settle soon. "Backseat, baby." Bullets, boys. Mom and Mom and Mom is mine.

Al's blue shirt goes in hamper in the bathroom. Glasses in the kitchen cupboard. "Pick up the room," Mom says and doing as she asks to please her. She is coming home. All alone for one whole day the first time ever. Old enough to skip the visits? Don't believe it but she says it's true and so it is. Try to make her happy with the cleaning make her smile when she gets back.

Picking up the room imagine lifting it with two bare hands. Bigger stronger house in hands and lifting it towards the sky. Looking down can see the bullets lying on the dusty road. No more boys they scatter through the fields like ants from this far up. Eyes that follow gravel road to smooth and black and broken lines. Eyes that follow lines to fields and follow fields to cities high. Looking farther still and far beyond and up and up and up and up. Lifting higher higher power angels there is here and now.

James Rae

Dance of the Serpent

I long for clouds. The sky-blue iridescence clings too close for comfort, like the mirror this morning: my cheeks thinned to airmail parchment, finely veined in blue. I revamped their vigour with a pat of rouge. Youth restored. The sky too I alter, splashing the blue beyond with tarnished silver in my mind's eye. Better. This is how I will paint it, as an old woman's tattered cloak.

I suppress a shiver and notice my troika of émigré friends arriving: moon-faced Oksana, Sophia peering over her half spectacles, and Oleana in an unflattering striped sweater, her tummy bulging alarmingly. I wait, fatigued. My mantra for the past months loops incessantly in my mind's ear, "He will never leave." I stiffen inwardly and force myself to smile, trying to supplant it with a new chant, "One of them will want him."

The past six months with Sacha have been a trial. Today he will dance. He dances so well. I will be delivered.

Do they see me breaking a sweat? They mustn't. Smile, Erika, there is nothing to fear ... In a fantasy I decided to wear my violet, green, and black dress, but at the last minute threw on a bulky turtleneck – a brisk wind off the lake vindicates my choice, unbecoming as it may be for the occasion.

I welcomed Sacha into my home as a favour to Vivica, when their "business" ended. From the first, we decided on a "platonic relationship," and truly I couldn't imagine finding comfort in his wire-twist arms. He settled into father's old room, laying out his socks and underwear as neat and prim as a little girl. When I tiptoe in, the room is clean, betraying nothing of his malevolent odour.

At first I wanted him there, flattered by his youth, his searching gaze. Perhaps I want him still. But not his touch. Nobody knows. He can't help himself. I can see my son, Oli, wondering about us when he comes to visit. Luckily, Sacha resists his theatrical urge and lurks in his room until Oli leaves. Those times are the worst. His mere touch on my wrist ready to coil tight at any moment, his demands to know what I said and what Oli thought. I always reassure him, but am seldom believed. Sometimes it is only a slap. And the things he says ... but I understand his cruelty, our secret. I see how sensitive Sacha is, how easily hurt. His life has not been easy. But now I know this must end.

On her husband Bartov's arm, clown-faced Oksana advances, her fox stole hiding her chins. I glimpse a flash of green – Sacha's costume – and glance away. Oksana tells me he spoke to her of the music I laboured to select. Perhaps she has been charmed? And there is so much work to do on their house – Sacha's handyman skills would surely be an asset.

Already, Sacha's long strides adopt a dance-like quality, as he places loudspeakers by the begonias. Vivica holds court in a clutch of émigrés. She is hosting this performance as a favour to me, perhaps she understands, though she doesn't let on. I weigh the odds, despite their feigned disinterest. "The same school as Nureyev," I remind them, unsure of the truth even now. I must still believe in fairy tales.

His long ponytail writhes in the verdant green of the garden, his lime-flecked leotards leave nothing of his maleness to the imagination. Better that way. Let one of them recoup lost youth. My seventy-odd years have taught me a thing or two. I long only for the solitude to mess in my paints without a nagging excitation, without a hanging threat.

"Scriabin, an astute choice, commands respect from the first half note," I say. And it is true. The crowd draws near. Sacha's long arms arc overhead, encompassing the heavens – and a tiny cloud that has lost its way – I note with a clandestine smile. Lest Sacha should think it is for him, I let my eyes go blank. And so the dance begins.

Baryshnikov himself would have been seduced, Nureyev would have been jealous. Sacha's slow, prancing circling tautens into a spin. In a sudden writhing I see the pain of my childhood nightmares, the Devil King of Russian fairy tales, and then, without warning, a man's body riddled with bullets under the cedars at the dacha – blood-hued dew in the same garden where frogs collected a little Princess's errant arrows of love.

My gasp goes unnoticed, caught up in the communal echo. Oksana looks transfixed – will she be the one? Or Sophia perhaps ... who would have thought? Arms clutched to her breasts, she looks ready to tear off her blouse and leap into the fray. Damn the buttons, Sophia, you can sew them back on later!

I have seen my share of dances – sweet Vladimir, my dear husband, departed so long ago – light-footed on the temple steps in Agrigente. Garden dances under cypress and cedar, oak and chestnut. Paris with war hastening on the wind, pure abandon, pure ... Hell and heaven under the same blue, too-blue sky.

Sacha's dance is all that and more, it is spiritual. He told me he rehearsed, but I suspect now he is improvising, caught up in something greater. Even the wind seems to abate, teasing the leaves to his rhythm. My cheeks burn. Sacha's coiled sinew loops and contorts. He is so young and ageless, still lithe and pliant, not yet fifty. It isn't fair, I have lived and loved, now I want to be left alone.

Veronika, a late arrival, hovers under the shade of the gable, impervious to the cold. Why not? She is strong-boned and confident. He would be putty in her hands, and she in his. He wouldn't hurt her then, not if he were happy.

Now he slithers, serpent-like, swallowing his prey, gorging on grass to help digest it. Every gesture, every pulse in perfect harmony with his chosen theme of transcendence and triumph. Sacha is one with his spirit. I feel him reaching for my inner darkness ... reach for theirs, Sacha, reach for theirs ...

Collapsing in the pansies, he clutches a red rose to his side, draws black blood from a finger – the shock of a wounded Christ, pure inspiration torn from the flowers, the trees, and the boundless cobalt sky. Please, Veronika, there is still time. Steal him, steal my young lover away. You're still young. He won't mind you're extra plump. Be soft ... he will be gentle. Look, see how he writhes so languidly in his throes? See what I see.

When my son Oli was little we danced circles, heads thrown back in Rings around the Rosies until we fell dizzy – heavy headed, but giddy nonetheless.

I hinted to Oli about my problem with Sacha, how I couldn't get him to go, or let him, and how I resented having my life and home invaded by his presence, his odour. I couldn't bear to even hint at the rest of it, and I always wrapped my arms and neck in a woollen shawl – just an old woman's affectation – even in the summer heat. Oli simply shrugged – not what you'd expect of a son you'd danced with in the park. The same boy who plucked flower petals and befriended bugs is so serious now. "You invited him in. Ask him to leave, he'll go," was all he said, never thinking to ask: go where?

The dance ends, to resounding applause. A stupendous success! Seeing Sophia's glow, I pin my hopes on her. But ... I'm not sure.

Oksana is nowhere to be seen. Is she off congratulating him? Her docile Bartov waxes effusively, "I admire the parallels, a great sensibility at work, hovering on the sexual yet never maudlin ... Very moving." I concur, pressing on, seeking out my saviour. I soon see on hushed, evasive faces that none will emerge. Vivica whispers forgiveness for her flowerbeds, and it is over. I gambled and lost. But so did he.

In the week that follows, Sacha complains to me – a hint of desperation in his voice – that nobody will hire him anymore. Maybe his clients were afraid of his depth of passion? What can he do? I try to soothe him. I hear him swear under his breath, but soon the hiss subsides.

So the dance wasn't a success, maybe it is foolish for a greying man in a ponytail to prance in lime-green leotards before a group of dried old prunes. I wait until he relaxes his stare, and I continue, plotting as I speak, "With Oli's help we can find you a camera."

"I can use your studio."

I swallow and hasten to reply, afraid to upset him, "Yes, my studio."

"Patience Erika" is my new mantra. Of course, now there is no choice, he must stay. In some ways I am glad. I do not want the serpent dance to end.

I think often of dear Vladimir, now a saint in my memories. Silently I thank Sacha for that, he doesn't mean to be cruel. It is only his nature.

Yes, I am an old woman, but I don't want the dance to end. His blood runs cold, I can feel it. His slit eyes don't see me, or feel me drying to a burnt husk with his every touch. I am consumed.

If only he didn't smell so ... malevolent. It isn't that he doesn't wash. When I tiptoe into his room, it is very clean, all his underwear and socks lined up just like a little girl's. The odour is not his fault. It is in his nature. And I, I am an old woman, what am I to do? What have I done?

Willa and Iris on the Monday before Christmas

"Oh, And I'll have a spot of that gravy, Willa, would you be a dear?"

"I'm sorry Iris, I didn't notice that you hadn't any."

"This is simply a work of art, Willa."

"Oh, don't be silly, Iris. It's a regular Monday dinner. I do love lamb though, don't you?"

"Yes, dear, I certainly do. Oh! Do you see Mrs. Harrison walking along by the bank there? My, she looks wonderful, cheeks as pink as a pale flamingo and that hair! I do say! I'm glad to know who her hairdresser is!"

"Oh yes. I rather liked it better before, Iris. She seems to have so much that it looks top heavy. Good thing it isn't windy, if you take my meaning!"

"Mm. Yes, I expect I do, dear. My, this lamb is cooked to perfection, so tender you could cut it with a fork, just like Mother's! And you add a cup of wine to the gravy, don't you? You simply couldn't buy a meal this delicious anywhere in Montreal, anywhere at all, I expect."

"You do go on, Iris."

"I feel very lucky, dear, that's all, not to have to eat that drudgery that I had in that terrible convalescent home … it was good of you to take me under your wing, Willa. I want you know that I continue to appreciate all your gourmet meals."

"You know, it's almost seven years now, since you moved here. Eight since Charlie died. And twelve since your Arthur passed away, good Heavens, time does fly. Well, I feel lucky not to have to handle a single dish!"

"You always did, dear, didn't you? I do so love to have a candle lit at dinner. No-one else does that except at Christmas and once at Mable's and Whendale's for their fortieth wedding anniversary. It makes a meal a meal, in my humble opinion."

"I quite agree. Iris, what are we going to do when the postman wakes up?"

"Well we tell him he fell asleep just as he did, indeed."

"Yes, but surely he'll wonder, like that young fellow, Mr. Pitkiern did the time before last."

"Did you reseal them all well this time?"

"Oh yes, that glue stick is a wonder, Iris."

"Well then I see no reason what so ever to worry or fret. I think it will be just fine, dear. They're all back in his bag and carefully sealed ... Mr. Pitkiern only worried that he might be having a heart attack or something ... nothing about the mail, dear. I'll go and put the kettle on and get the coffee started. Did you want to put ice cream on that apple crisp?"

"No, just plain, thanks – you know, with all the excitement ... I ought not, I think."

"Alright, dear, I'm having some. Good thing it's only once a year, eh Willa?"

"Oh dear, yes. Where did we get this lovely dish, Iris? "

"Oh, don't you remember when the minister and Mrs. Harvey and Gracey came for tea? Mrs. Harvey brought a lovely fruit salad in it, and I liked the dish so much that I put it on the sideboard and put candy peppermints in it. I offered you one last night before that television program."

"I guess that's why she ordered a new one from Sears, poor dear."

"Yes. And just imagine Eleanor ordering size 7 waist for a skirt."

"Maybe it's not for her at all – maybe it's for Nancy."

"But she already sent that lovely card and the twenty dollar cheque!"

"Oh, yes, that's right, well ..."

"Here's the cream, Willa. Perhaps we should send Nancy a birthday card."

"Then they would wonder how we knew, Iris."

"Of course they would! What a silly! I wouldn't make a very artful criminal would I? Too bad about that Robert fellow; imagine, $450 for a speeding ticket. Hope he learns his lesson."

"Yes. And Edna won't be attending the Fall Bridge Party if she is offered a chance to go up to Toronto, to Dean and Elsie's will she? We'll have to get a new partner!"

"I expect so, dear. I expect so."

"We ought to save some of this crisp for the postman don't you think? It said on the bottle to be taken with a meal. Do hope it doesn't bother his stomach."

"Oh no, he's quite a young man and by the looks of things in very good condition, I would say! I've seen him drinking Coca-Cola. If he drinks that, well dear, I'm sure he could stomach just about anything."

"Here's to your marvellous idea, Iris. Keeps us in touch with our community doesn't it, dear? Now that we are too old and frail to get about. Cheers!"

ANDY BROWN

Sleeves Sewn Shut

I drove the school bus even though I was only thirteen. My father was the town's mechanic, so everyone assumed I knew what I was doing. Some of the kids I drove to the high school were much older than me. I sat on a thick copy of *Fishes of the World* to see over the yellow hood. At home I kept a notebook where I copied out the lines of fins, drawing scales and eyeballs.

My mother had little need for clocks that were not inherited. The only thing she desired was to live in the city, but my father had lied to her before they had been married. It wasn't until after the ceremony that she discovered he was a mechanic in a small town. They moved in above the garage and had me.

My father would sometimes take me hunting in the afternoons. Mostly for ducks. He wouldn't kill anything he was unwilling to eat, and without refrigeration, killing moose or deer seemed excessive.

My father was walking ahead of me, his eyes searching the long grass. There were rifles suspended under our arms. The metal of the rifle rubbed against my armpit like a coin in a pocket. My father was obsessing over the ghosts hiding in the shadows of the grass. Sometimes a duck burst forth and pulled towards the sky before he lifted the rifle to his shoulder. He still had his hair, and it was forever getting in his eyes. He blew a loose strand from his face and took aim. He raised the gun to his eye and the grass bent with a slight shock. The duck shuddered in mid-air, a piece of meat erupting from its side.

My father lowered the rifle and flashed his yellow teeth at me. The duck lay crumpled like a woman's abandoned glove.

"Fine shot, Pa."

"Gotta always keep your eye ready."

He had worked on hundreds of cars before, but it was not until after the accident that he came to understand their engines: his concentration over gears, the viscosity between his fingers, the fetal scents of gasoline. He kept a pencil behind his ear, and, when he went to write out a receipt, he would always leave a black smudge just below his hairline.

I had seen my father kill before. Sometimes I would lie down in the grass, disappear, and watch him retrieve his kill and hold it over his shoulder. As evidence, not glory. He wanted me to be a witness, but I would be hiding in the dry grass, which was stiff and sharp like paper. Driving the school bus had given me a sense of independence. I was beginning to understand roads and where they could take you.

That morning he didn't come looking for me. He continued to scour the fields. When he came to a fence, he leaned his rifle on the other side, grabbed the wooden railing, and pulled himself over.

It was then that I heard it.

I stood up, emerging from the moment as if stepping out of a photograph.

The blade of grass fell from my mouth as I ran.

My father was clutching the end of his arm, his hand had become the accumulation of those lost pieces of meat flying out of ducks. His arm hung from his body like a comma on a blank page. His face was rigid and calm. He was on a boat in the middle of Beaver Lake, falling asleep watching his fishing line cut into the water. He was in a state of shock.

Pieces of his hand hid under the slivers of the fence. The rifle was still warm when I picked it up. I didn't understand why I felt the need to pick up the fallen rifle and lean it against the fence before I said anything.

"Pa! Oh my God, Pa."

"I should'a known better."

"We have to do something."

"Give me your shirt."

I gave him my shirt and with surprising strength, considering the circumstances, he ripped off a sleeve with his teeth. He wrapped it around the end of his arm. It was disturbing how calm he was.

"Pull this tight."

I quickly put my torn shirt back on, fumbling with the buttons, conscious of my naked arm. I cradled both rifles under it as we made our way back across the field. The two guns were dancing just above the tips of the grass. My father's face was filled with lines, as if his pain had been drawn on him. I wanted to hold his hand for comfort, but there was an absence at the end of his arm as we ran, staggering with the weight of accident.

I drove the school bus into the closest town with a hospital. My father lay on the back seat of the bus moaning. Every time we hit a bump his entire body would be suspended off the seat. In the rear view mirror he looked like a helpless volunteer from the audience being levitated by a magician.

Because I was driving so fast and was unfamiliar with speed at that age, I almost lost control of the bus when I hit a pothole. There was a loud noise before it began to lose power. My father yelled something from the back about pulling over.

On the side of the road, I opened the hood for him. Birds left the earth around us. My father reached into the engine with his only hand. A piece of bloody cloth dangled from his other arm, which he held over his head. I could make out a cuff stitched into the cloth. He maneuvered and twisted his arm through the engine like a question mark. The ends of his hair drooped over his eye, dipping into ink. He was writing that engine.

"Maybe you should put another bandage on. That one's pretty red."

"In a minute." He was breathing hard.

He finished with the engine and pulled his hand out gingerly. I drove the bus the rest of the way to the hospital.

When my mother found out, she assumed the family would finally move to the city. Instead we stayed above the garage, and my father became notoriously popular as the only one-handed mechanic in the province. People would bring their Packards from miles around. My mother sewed shut the left sleeve on all his shirts. The black smudges remained above his ear for days before eventually being wiped off.

Patrick Allard

A Moment near Solo

Ghostly voices from unseen mosques wake me. The first call to prayer wafts in through the open windows of the eastbound train.

We reach the city's outskirts. The train slows to a more traditional Javanese pace, the crawl. The sun rises quickly, as does the stench of open sewers. Out the window, to the south, I see an endless stream of corrugated iron huts, half-hidden by shrubbery and assorted fruit trees – papaya mostly. And garbage. Smouldering, reeking piles of it sprawl everywhere, consuming the landscape. To the north, muddy paddy fields extend perhaps a hundred yards, before merging into a grey mist. Thus the rainy season begins; the early morning sun bakes the mud and sleeping water buffalo, as it summons moisture into the air. The earth, reluctant to let go after so many arid months, defends itself with an armour of steam that hovers until late morning, when the clouds, unable to resist, douse the land with rain. This daily battle between sky and earth has its own scent, one I welcome, for it marks my return to the city I love, my home, so far from home.

Careful not to wake the old Bapak and his prized fighting cock asleep at my feet, I walk towards the lavatory, eager to relieve an anxious bladder brimming with the coconut water I've drunk throughout the long, tedious journey from the capital. I don't like it much anymore, but, unlike other questionable liquids peddled onboard, I can trust it.

The Indonesian train-lavatory is a loathsome beast, better feared from afar. The best approach is no approach, but if you must draw near, be cautious. Partitioned from the rest of the coach, it's next to, and level with, the top of a two-and-a-half-foot high boarding step. Negotiating the toilet's entrance without stumbling onto the step, and perhaps off the train, requires excellent balance. It's a death trap at night when drunk or unawares, for the lights rarely work. Even more unsettling is the ooze that seeps from its bowels, ever ready to sully the hand of any passenger who uses the edge of the lavatory floor to pull himself aboard.

Indonesian trains were designed for Europe, where stations have elevated platforms. In the Archipelago, only Jakarta has this feature. Everywhere else platforms are at track level, making the first step huge, even for a giant *bulé* (white man) like me. Indonesians, like most Asians, are short, making boarding even more challenging. What they lack in height, though, they more than make up for with grace, flexibility, and good humour, especially the old women. One would think them unable to board at all, with their tightly wrapped sarongs and narrow gait, but they usually manage. On rare occasions when they don't, they'll collar a stranger, demand a push, then giggle like schoolgirls as they're shoved aboard.

On all the local trains I've ridden, exit doors are bolted open to avoid jamming during the boarding chaos. Wind rushing between them has supplied the only fresh air (or at least illusion of it) I've encountered during my six years here, but this train's moving too slowly to generate any breeze at all. Halfway to my destination, the stench from the "weh ceh" (as they pronounce it here) overpowers me. I pause where the wagons join, one foot on the wagon ahead, one on the wagon behind. It occurs to me to wait until we arrive, but I really must pee. Ahead, I notice a soldier standing on the lower step, facing the rice fields. He's not holding on – precarious, foolish I feel, even at this speed. Then I see; he's urinating. If he can pee out the door, so can I.

I don't want to interrupt, so I stand, barely moving. When he's done, I'll exchange pleasantries then follow in his footsteps, his puddles. (Peeing from moving trains can be sloshy.) The constant "ke-klak" and metallic screech hides me. I wait quietly, astride the chasm, above the moving tracks.

There are moments, while travelling, when I feel freedom from what was and what will be. I've always cherished these moments. This, however, is not one of them.

I ponder discussions I've had, inner searchings that led me to this journey. From the beginning I've been shaky regarding the thing I'm hours from doing. Perversely, I now experience these sensations physically. My "conversion" to Islam, prerequisite for marrying my Javanese princess, is bereft of spiritual content and torments no-one, apparently, but me. That the process is per-functory, that everyone involved expects as much, doesn't reconcile the hypocrisy I feel. Java: land of a thousand masks. I am barely comfortable with the mask I'm wearing. This sense of rupture has intensified recently. If the train were to come apart where I stand, I'd remain there, split by indecision.

I don't notice the soldier behind me. He taps my shoulder. I jump, try to turn. My balance goes. I stumble across him.

"Maaf, Pak," I apologize.

"No what what!" He grins.

Empty questions, which custom requires, will follow, questions I'll respond to with equally empty answers. I'm not in the mood, but I did, after all, trip over him.

"Where are you from, bulé?"

"Saya dari Canada," I reply.

"Where are you going?"

I hide my annoyance at this enquiry, posed on a train ten minutes from Solo-Belapan, the final stop. I say it's my destination. I grow restless as I wait for the big question.

"Agama apa, bulé?" What's your religion?, he asks.

The first few times, while still an innocent backpacker, I'd tried to answer honestly, to speak of my spiritual rather than religious relationship with God. But I'd soon learned my answer wouldn't do. The interrogator, confused, would ask again. If I persisted, conversation would cease, often with a final, derogatory remark thrown my way. *Saya katolik* became my response. It made everyone happy.

I respond to the soldier. "*Besok saya mau masok Islam. Tahun depan saya lagi kawin.*" Tomorrow I become Muslim. I'll marry next year.

I've opened up to a stranger, shared my torment, and now I'm sorry I have. I know I've encouraged conversation, something I'm unprepared for. I know little of the Koran. Any question about things Muslim will expose me. Then, without raising an eyebrow, he says, "Good, good!" and he's on his way – just like that.

I have to pee. Three paces and I'm on the ledge where he'd stood, relief washes over me (and my shoes). I review thoughts of being split, of my exchange with the soldier. I'd expected a symphony to "conversion," a barrage of questions about my betrothed and her family. That they hadn't been asked has left a void – I've been changed.

The stench from the toilet ebbs. Then like the nutty smell of earth that rises from passing fields, meaning comes. To stand on shaky ground in life, as on a train, has been my choice. I recall what I'd once known but forgotten, that I'm powerless over trains and their motives. So why argue if it takes me someplace I love? I find my moment, and I'm pleased.

A Loaded Donkey

Who can say how these things start? There's never any reason per se that I can point to. It isn't like I can pin it on this or that and say there was something definite. Take yesterday for instance.

I come in feeling busted, my back screaming, and go heat up some milk. I heat it up and stir in some honey. All this time Janet's on the couch and we haven't spoken. I bring the mug over to the couch and sit down next to her. I just want to talk of nice things – small-talk – nothing that's going to get me thinking. It's one of those early morning dreams I want; one of those dreams where everything's completely wonderful and nothing's lacking. It's a sense of well-being you just don't have when you're awake. Whatever the events are, they drift along in a warm shifting light. Nothing is lacking until something wakes you and the longing sets in. Consciousness sits on you like a germ. It's strange that things are never reversed and waking saves you from something. Only once I dreamt sharks were chasing me, but I'd mastered them by the end and, before I awoke, we were swimming together.

Anyway, that's how things should be – easy like that, pleasant like that. So now she has the Discovery Channel on, and they're covering armadillos. This is a good start. I take up a lock of her hair and stare at it. I smell it. It smells like peaches. She turns suddenly and tightens her brow, staring indignantly. I smile and offer her my milk. She shakes her head and turns back to the TV.

Silence is okay, it's good, nothing bad can come of it. But after a while she gets up and says, "I have to call Pierre."

Now, Pierre is this gay man in town who she's not even friends with; what she could have with him is beyond me.

"Why?" I ask.

She looks at me over her shoulder. "Fashion design," she says on her way upstairs. "He has information."

I put my mug down, turn, and watch her disappear at the top. "Fashion design?" I call after her.

"He knows the schools," she says.

"What do you mean," I say, following her up. I stand in the doorway to our room as she goes through her organizer.

"I mean, I'm gonna study design." She dials with the receiver pinched between her chin and shoulder. I just stand there and look at her. She has her head up against the wall and taps a pencil impatiently on the table. There's no answer, and she sighs, lowering the phone.

I go over and touch her elbow. "We're done with school," I say.

She looks at me and laughs this tired, almost angry laugh. "You think I'm going to go on in this dead-end job, don't you? Well I'm not. I hate my life."

"You're just starting ... It'll get better."

"Pff!" she exclaims.

"Besides," I say, "I don't think there's anywhere in Montreal that offers that."

"Did I say Montreal?"

"Why are you talking like this? We can't leave, we've got rent to pay and my mother, you know how she is. Janet, I have to look after her. And God, you think I work that job for fun? Look, we're just starting out ..."

"I didn't say you had to come."

"Come on, Janet, don't talk like this. You can't go off and ..."

"You're in for a surprise, big guy, if you think I'm gonna keep that desk job."

"Janet, you can't go. We'll figure something out."

"So I'm supposed to rot here and do whatever you want?"

I put my arms around her and she pulls away, goes over by

the window. I wait a moment and follow, pressing my face in her hair. I reach down by her belt.

"Stop!" she says, jerking away. "You're so ... clingy."

She uses this word, clingy. Her face has reddened, and she stands there with her arms up tight against her chest, staring at me. When I move forward, she bursts out crying and rushes into the bathroom.

I stand outside the door, knowing it's locked, and listen to her quiver. I hear muffled blubbering and things being moved around on the counter. What can I say that I haven't already? I don't know how things got to this. I mean, there was a time when we didn't need anything else. Can I remind her of this? – that we didn't need anything or anyone. I don't even know how to begin.

I go downstairs, pour a glass of water and sit at the kitchen table. It's getting dark outside and there's a rising wind whistling as it bends over the eave. I sit listening to this, turn the lamp on, and stare at it. It feels cool in the room, and I reach up and adjust the thermostat.

After a time I hear movement above, then slow footsteps on the stairs. She enters the kitchen in high heels and a dress she'd made: a beautiful long ochre affair in crinkled polyester. Her hair is tied back, and her watery eyes gleam from her make-up. If only she'd give a hint of a smile, that's all, just to show things are right.

"Don't," she says as I approach her.

I go over and lower my head against her chest. I can feel her trembling. I look in her face and she's biting her lip; tears are beading up.

It's crazy, I know, but I tell her this story. It's a story my grandfather used to tell. Back in the thirties, in Drummondville, he worked in a textile plant, and the view from his desk was of the storage yard. One day he noticed a donkey saddled with a huge wicker basket full of bricks. The donkey could barely walk with such a burden; it teetered and stumbled forward, falling to its knees. Beside the donkey there was a small man driving it on with a whip. My grandfather went out and told the man to stop, saying the donkey could not go on. He put it simply like that, saying it was just too much. The guy was wooden and stared, unanswering. My grandfather went back inside, and, when he saw the man carrying on more brutally than ever, he returned to resolve the matter differently. My grandfather would smile at this, when he'd get to this part of the story. He never told what he had done, only saying that he used to have red hair, as if this explained everything. Enough is enough, he'd say.

When I finish talking, she pulls away and stares at me. She looks puzzled or accusing or both. It's unclear what I've done; she normally likes to hear stories like that.

"I'm going out," she says, getting her jacket from the coat-rack. I stand on the step watching her as she leaves the house. A light snow is falling, an autumn snow, and the wind whirls it round with the fallen leaves. And, with all of this blowing against her, she leaves the glow of the porch light, and her outline dims as she continues on to the car.

Feeding Him

I sit at his bedside. The wooden chair has a wobble in its joints. The seat is contoured, presumably buttock-shaped, but its curves don't fit mine. The awkward pressure against my pelvis threatens my leg with pins and needles. My new suede jacket is bundled in a graceless heap over the chair back – there was nowhere else to put it. Whenever I move, I am aware that the jacket might slip to the floor and be sullied by dust, cobwebs, god knows what unthinkable liquids may have spilled, fallen, or leaked on the ground.

The sweet stink of disinfectant is everywhere. I have gotten used to it. The nurse, however, has just brought in the lunch tray and awakened my nostrils to a barrage of new smells. Lima beans dominate, but the nasal assault includes perspiration and laundry soap from the nurse's uniform, turkey salad, the rotting stems of the flowers on the bedside cabinet, the goaty odour of disease, the smell of new leather from my own coat, and the ever-present disinfectant. I repress my nausea; it is mere self-indulgence.

I poke at the food with the fork. The lima beans are still steaming. Beside them is a hillock of something orange and mashed – is it squash? The turkey salad looks like an accident, irregular white lumps in a yellowish goo. The last pile must be the hospital's version of rice pilaf, with its reddish, greenish, and blackish specks among the grains.

He is propped up on the pillows, his mouth slightly agape, waiting. I twist into position. The bed rail grinds into my kneecap.

For the first forkful, the squash. It holds together in a lump and, though my arm is unsteady, I guide it towards the waiting aperture without any mishap. A delicate pressure against the fork

– it is empty. With the fork, I trace a map in the squash, a grid dividing it into six more bites. I count nineteen lima beans and guess I can manage four on the fork at a time. The math is simple – this will be five trips mouthward. The rice may be trickier. But now the moist, sucking noises of mastication have subsided. I spear the biggest chunk of turkey and approach again. I do not look at him; my aim is fairly accurate, although I am relying on my peripheral vision. I know, though, that the rice and beans will demand a more careful trajectory.

Chewing the turkey keeps him busy awhile, and I work through my strategy. I scoop a mound of rice onto the fork and trace figure eights in the air just above the plate. Nothing falls. The grains of the pilaf hold together nicely. I tip the rice off the fork and practice with the lima beans. Four, then five beans fit comfortably on the fork. Great, now I can get it down to (nineteen divided by five equals) four bean trips. I eye the rice again and determine that I have perhaps five rice trips. That makes five plus four plus, did I say six? Fifteen forkfuls. Then the five remaining turkey lumps brings it to twenty, a satisfying number. A telephone rings. I'm aware of the soft to-ing and fro-ing of the hospital staff in the corridor.

Silence from the bed signals time for another mouthful. I scoop up five beans, but lose one en route. It bounces off his torso, the edge of the bed, disappears from view. As I am focused on delivering the other four beans, I'll have to investigate its whereabouts later. Mission achieved. But, damnation. Fourteen beans left, and if it's to be just four beans per trip, that's three bean trips and two beans remaining. Perhaps I can spear one bean with each of two lumps of turkey?

Back to the squash, thrice in a row. It is a reliable food, not willful like beans or rice. My right shoulder blade aches. It'd be easier if I sat on the bed itself, but a dim childhood memory says that this is against the rules, although I cannot imagine that these hurrying nurses would bother to chastise me. More honestly, I know I cannot deal with this feeding task face on. Eating is an appalling activity, best done in privacy or with the distractions of music or clever conversation to shield witnesses from its vulgarity.

Watching him eat – seeing the gratitude and anger in his pale eyes – would be intolerable.

I switch to my left hand to rest my right shoulder. My left elbow clumsily knocks against the bedrail, and, though the food eventually ends up in the correct place, a brief glance shows the yellow smudge of sauce on his chin. I shift the chair slightly, pinning my suede coat against the chair back with my left forearm so that the coat will not fall. A ray of sunlight catches my shirt sleeve. The room is hot; my armpits and toes are sticky; but this spot of sunshine flickers as the trees move, plays over the stripes of my shirt – cheers me.

I shrug and roll my shoulders to relieve the cramped muscles. Right hand again. The rapid disappearance of the squash is gratifying and I'm making real inroads into the rice. Soon, however, my shoulder is howling in protest. I squirm, grimace, and press on, calculating again. Two turkeys, two rice, two bean trips left to go. I'll leave the two extra beans on the plate "for Miss Manners."

I'll deliver these six forkfuls in reverse alphabetical order, then repeat: turkey, rice, beans, turkey, rice, beans. I spear the turkey, stretch ... and meet resistance. My eyes jerk up in surprise. His mouth is pressed shut. His eyes are closed. A new yellow smear on his lips matches the old, coagulating one on his chin. My arm, fork, and turkey lump hover uncertainly in midair. I lower the fork. Okay, no more turkey. I use the edge of the plate to slide the lump off the tines. Lacking an alternative, I decide to stick with my strategic plan, so I take a scoop of rice and raise the fork to his lips.

There is no strength in his thin white arm, but the fact of the blow stuns me. Not to mention the explosion of rice, a greasy confetti on the bed, on my shirt, on the floor. I feel a hot sting at the back of my eyes. Still clutching the fork, I push back the chair and stand up. Pins and needles bristle as the blood rushes into my feet. On my first step away from the bedside, I feel the slippery grains of rice underfoot. On my next step I tread heavily on my new suede coat, which has fallen to the floor. I stoop to pick it up – the soft leather bears the pattern of my shoe sole, dotted with the mashed larvae of rice. I want to hurl the fork across the room; my arm tenses, anticipating the movement, exulting in it. Instead I turn back and lay the fork carefully on the tray. I speak. My voice sounds high and thin to my ears, but surprisingly steady: "Goodbye, Freddy. See you tomorrow."

He opens his eyes and regards me impassively. "Yes," he says.

COLIN MACWHIRTER

Interior

Reassembling the salvaged woodwork of a tiny turn-of-the-century chapel condemned after the 1989 earthquake, Porter Duncan has created a San Francisco high-rise sanctuary ... Arched oak paneling forms a Gothic colonnade in the entrance hall, lightened by a sky-blue ceiling. Two stained glass windows color the living room with scenes of John the Baptist and Lazarus arisen from the dead. They were the only windows to survive the quake and did so, miraculously, entirely undamaged. Two other treasures rescued from the quake, a pair of hymn boards, flank the doorway to the room of Duncan's butler.

–Design & Decoration, March 1999

There was almost no sound in the apartment ... only a bristling, brushing sound. The sound of Erickson polishing a pair of black boots. Now they were perfect for this evening.

Erickson put the polishing supplies back in their designated bright red tool box, put the tool box back on the shelf of his work closet, next to the iron and the starch bottle – Mr. Duncan liked his collars crisp. There was little else to do for now. He laid the selected suit out on the bed – with a choice of two neckties – and noiselessly walked to the kitchen to finish making a pre-outing snack: two mushroom and chicken liver tarts. The tarts in the oven, he could open the letter from his mother.

He still hadn't decided whether his mother was senile or merely eccentric. Nothing to do with the red whirly handwriting on the envelope nor the offhand elliptical return address: Erickson, Carlyle, Sask. It was that she persisted, in spite of his frequent corrections, in imagining him as an executive assistant. Sometimes he thought she might be mocking him, not taking his position seriously. Certainly, she couldn't understand that, for him, southern Saskatchewan was bland disorder. But neither her ignorance, if that's what it was, nor any taunting could displace him from his well-fitting niche.

My dear Derek, he read, *I imagine you're well, as always. I've found it a bit windy for my liking recently, giving me a bit of a sniffle, but M. Keller assures me Spring is on the way – he can tell from the way his cattle are lowing, I expect. Of course, I never did pay enough attention to such points of animal husbandry. How are you faring with that Mr. Duncan of yours? Why don't you let somebody else take over some of the paperwork you're always smothering in so you can visit for a week? We'll borrow your uncle and his car and drive out to the Cypress Hills. Well, I'll be off – mending the screen door – Spring brings flies. Drop me a note. Love, Mom.* He folded the letter into its envelope and placed it next to several others in the drawer of his bedside table.

The apartment door had closed behind Mr. Duncan and his footfalls echoed down the hall. Erickson poured a glass of wine, placed it next to the plate of tarts on the table. Mr. Duncan sat, pulling the napkin from its coiled silver ring.

As Mr. Duncan ate, Erickson provided a selection of newspapers, turned up the lighting slightly, and refilled the wine glass – his movements circling smoothly round those of Mr. Duncan so that the two men performed a wordless choreography. This was not design but mutual proprioception, the fruit of habit and two neatly compatible demeanours.

So another two hours passed without more than a word between them, while Mr. Duncan undressed, groomed himself, and dressed – Erickson helping him, fixing his collar, for example.

As he closed the heavy dark door behind Mr. Duncan,

Erickson saw again the reflection of his employer in the antique bedroom mirror: Mr. Duncan reviewing his own appearance, unmindful of Erickson's alert gaze. The image hung over Erickson for a minute or two as he sat in the kitchen to eat his own supper of greens, an avocado, and rice. Mr. Duncan didn't approve of vegetarianism, considering it an affectation.

Erickson scanned the Examiner, his fork occasionally clinking against the plate.

It was late in the party, a gathering of thirty or so friends Porter Duncan had come to know through his interest in art and collecting – he didn't have work friends. It was late in the party, a time when certain voices boomed loudly over the music, over others nearly hushed.

Porter, who drank steadily but without apparent drunkenness, was deep in conversation with the only person present he'd never met before, someone he'd been warned against: "She'll eat you alive, Porter. Don't worry about it. And don't think of asking her out for 'coffee.'" He found this sort of advice insulting, not helpful. Anyway, it hardly mattered because they found each other anyway. He thought her original and delightful. Obviously, she'd been told something about him because she was grilling him about his work as a civil engineer – he was quite happy to fill her in. Then she changed her tack.

"I understand you have a live-in manservant or whatever. What's the deal with that?"

"Erickson is indispensable. He makes my life possible. He maintains the order I require to function. In return, I provide for him."

"You couldn't just live together, pool resources. Instead, it's two men living intimately together with this unbreachable economic barrier."

"Well, of course it's not just economics. I depend on his

judgment–"

"Like, 'which tie should I wear …?'"

"He has excellent taste, sartorially."

And on it went for a while, till it was clear to them both that there were no more corners worth exploring.

Though, returning home, her words – it could only have been the aftereffects of liquor – her words, echoing in his mind, accompanied memories of Erickson coming to him, of Erickson's well-tailored letter in response to the ad in the paper. Porter found himself wondering how, indeed, would a man make his way from the Canadian Prairies to the Bay and deliver himself into an uncommon and presumably doubt-inspiring employment? It was not a question to which he had an answer. He was simply glad of the outcome.

Looking out at the appalling, huge sky, Adele considered again her son's peculiar little life while she gripped – maybe a little too firmly – one of his letters in her hand. She understood something of his loathing for this landscape; she found it austere and suspected he found it vertiginous. But she could see he'd grown up convinced of the superiority of urban society. She could see he believed in the rightness of caste, and clearly he was content to keep his place attending the Brahmins. It was, maybe, an inverted chivalry. Certainly, he'd been a fussy child, fastidious really, and now he, himself, fulfilled his rule: a place for everything …

The tone of his letter suggested he was hurt; he didn't seem to appreciate her sense of irony, but she couldn't help teasing him. Doing so diverted her from the feeling of disappointment.

Now that Mr. Duncan had returned, comfort returned. The bedside clock said three a.m. Peace in the secular chapel, the sanctified penthouse.

Touch Me

I set out to walk to the depanneur, but the closer I got the greater became the temptation to buy the book I'd noticed in the bookstore just a bit further on. I confess, the thought of another week of lentil stew did cause me to hesitate outside the depanneur before passing it by. And, when I discovered the entrance to the bookstore blocked by a portly woman fishing for change to pay for her books, I almost turned back. But I felt obliged to enter after exchanging glances with the old guy wearing the beret who perched just inside the door behind his antique cash register. The woman said, "If you get any more books in here, you'll go out of business!" True enough, yawning cats basked in dust-laden sunbeams on boxes of books in the window, and stacks of books covered almost all the open floor between the bookshelves. I browsed contentedly in the sunlight and muffled street noise for perhaps an hour before moving back into the gloom of the Philosophy section.

First the phone rang then I heard a female voice vying for the attention of the old guy at the cash who'd just answered it. The clear voice – she must have had training – repeated that she'd forgotten the keys to her bike lock, and would he please keep his eye on her bicycle while she went inside. But he stubbornly continued talking into the phone, even raising his voice to drown her out. I understood from a gruff and irritable "Alright already!" that he'd understood her. As I leafed through a book I was aware of her picking her way down the narrow aisle toward the back of the store. Curious to see what the owner of such a voice could look like, I glanced up and directly into a pair of amused, intelligent eyes beyond the young man who stood between us. I impassively lowered my gaze to my book. Seconds later and close behind me her voice said brightly, "Excuse me!" in response to which I leaned over the pile of books at my feet, steadied myself on a shelf, and allowed her to brush past nimbly. She stood too close to me and studied the Philosophy section also. The young man in front of us moved on to Science Fiction.

The old guy explained into the phone, "... some babe and her bike ..." and when he said, "... forgot her keys ..." she tossed her hair in my direction and chirped, "Silly me!" apparently for my benefit. I continued to turn pages, but no longer saw the words. In the periphery of my vision I saw her loop a strand of hair behind her ear with a finger and shoot me a sidelong smirk. She smelled of freshly ironed cotton, her smock came down to mid-thigh, and she wore sneakers with ankle socks. I still made no response. She shrugged, turned toward the shelves, hummed softly and ran her chewed index fingernail across each book spine, expertly flipping it toward her by crooking her finger as if beckoning to me. As her fingers came closer, I felt increasingly uncomfortable. I snapped my book shut when she reached the place on the shelf I'd taken it from. Saying nothing, I raised it deliberately in front of her. She froze. With a corner of my book, I arrogantly flipped back the last two books she'd moved and dropped mine into its place. Indignant, she stared straight at me. Suddenly struck by doubt, I felt my face redden as if it were too close to the arc of a search-light.

While I'd pretended to appraise my book, I imagined making contact with her, asking her exactly what she was looking for, saying that I made frequent rounds of the Philosophy sections in the neighbourhood's bookstores and that I could possibly tell her where she could find the book she wanted. But then I imagined us sitting together in a café awkwardly trying to find interests in common and trying to impress each other with our erudition. I thought I had recognized the aria she hummed, but my knowledge of opera was scanty; I was afraid of looking foolish, and I disliked that opera anyway. And I always hated myself after such show-and-tells for resorting to shocking personal revelations in a vain attempt at one-upmanship. Anyway, I couldn't afford to buy her a cup of coffee. And why bother? With such a voice and with such a forward attitude – both so clearly cultivated for effect – she's likely to be a pretentious, manipulative, possessive bitch. We'd be at each other's throats within a week. I doubt she's genuine, but ... But at that moment I simply had to escape her challenging, incendiary stare that demanded an explanation or apology.

After dropping my book back into place I retracted my hand like a robot. Avoiding her eyes, I pointlessly glanced over the books I'd picked, clamped them under my arm, and, without a word, turned to face her – but also in the direction of the cash – and waited. Our eyes met. She jutted her chin forward defiantly, prompting me, but her composure faltered when she understood my resolve. She frowned, barely perceptibly shook her head and uttered a faint but audible grunt of surprise and disgust. Why, I wondered, if she's genuinely intelligent, would she be so damn desperate to make contact with a complete stranger? She obliged me by turning and, on tip-toe, leaning over a box of books to flatten herself against the bookshelf to let me pass. It seemed an overtly theatrical gesture, and from the corner of my eye I noted that she seemed as vulnerable as if held in a pillory. Her smock had slid up her thighs a good three inches when she raised her arms. I was stepping carefully around her heels and the piles of books when I clearly heard her say, sotto-voce, "Touch me!"

It seemed like the universe blinked for a moment. A cold sweat broke on my back. I was blinded by a swirl of conflicting emotions. The bookstore blotted out entirely. The cash register seemed to be at the end of a very long dark tunnel. Part of me wanted to return to her, touch her, crush her into the musty books, mingle our breath, and bury my face in her hair. But my carcass moved angrily onward – affronted, dignified, and imperturbable – and I did nothing of the sort. The old guy at the cash had difficulty with his mental arithmetic, so I cleared my throat and did it for him. I paid for the books and, as I turned onto the sidewalk taking a deep breath of fresh air, I almost tripped over her bicycle. I hesitated outside the bookstore; that final lilt in her voice caromed around in my head. Was it a note of desperation, or was she mocking me? And, when I discovered my way blocked by a red light, I almost turned back. But, then it turned green, and, goaded on by the quizzical scrutiny of the advancing pedestrians, I felt obliged to continue.

Julia's List

You're saying she always wore black. You're saying she drank a tad too much. She gave you a Ken doll. You gave her a Barbie doll.

Months after I first found out, you're telling me this. In the dark, amid endless silences. You said then you'd never get into details. It was over between you and her.

But now I'm saying to you, in the silence that has fallen over us once more like a blight, "What was her name?"

Of course you're not going to tell, it wouldn't be like you. We'll just lie like this forever, your stubbly chin scraping my shoulder like a hair shirt, like sandpaper on an open sore.

But you actually give in.

"Her name's Michelle."

The banality of it enrages me once more. A triangle. Something not in my script. Till now my life had an outline. First, twenty years ago, we were Rob and Julia. Then, Rob, Julia, and Jennie. Then, Rob, Julia, Jennie, and Tamara. No, not quite. By then it was Julia, Rob, Jennie and Tamara, for times had changed.

You're telling me she's in computers, that she plays tennis. That's why it was okay. You weren't really lying. That's what the two of you did. Played tennis first.

First.

In the morning when I look in the mirror, I see the stunned eyes of a wronged woman. I can't believe I can look like this. I can't believe I can care this much.

When I first found out, you told me what you'd needed was to experience another woman. Because neither of us had ever been with anyone else. Because we went that far back. To high school.

But that's something I thought was special about us. That we went back that far.

Chump.

The weird thing is, sometimes things seem better between us. We're even making love again. I watch myself doing it with curiosity. The craving is stronger than ever, a new kind of wildness, even though I'm left hanging at the end. Because stretched between us like Clingwrap lie the pores of a stranger.

Michelle.

We sit side by side in swivel chairs faced by the therapist, a beautifully groomed woman whose nails match her cherry-painted lips. Another triangle.

"Look, when I called," I say, "I thought this was about a marriage going sour, some kind of mid-life thing. But since then I've discovered Rob's been having an affair–"

She looks at you. "Really?"

You nod.

"But you agreed to come."

You nod again.

"Why?"

"Julia said she'd leave me if I didn't. She did go away, and wouldn't come home unless I came here."

"And she didn't know then that you were seeing another woman?"

"No. She left because she claimed I was being impossible."

"Are you here against your will?"

I can barely make out your voice over the drone of the air conditioner.

"I'm here because Julia's my life."

Another time the therapist wears black. Her hair is pulled back in a chignon. Her nails and lips are mauve.

"Are you aware that you're angry at Julia?"

"I'm not angry at Julia. Julia's angry at me."

"What do you want from her?"

"Nothing."

"Julia's your life, and you want nothing from her? Can you explain that?"

"What he wants," I break in, "is *flattery*. That's what he tells me he got from this Michelle of his. *She* told him he was terrific. Why don't *I* say he's terrific? Do you believe he expects me to think he's *terrific* after this?

"Julia, Julia," the therapist soothes. "Let Rob tell it for himself."

Silence.

Today the therapist wears green leather. The lips and nails are coral.

"Why did you lie to Julia, Rob?"

Silence.

"Rob, I see a lot of couples. Some of them have open marriages. The woman comes home, the man comes home, they cook dinner together, she says to him, 'Guess what, hon? I met someone today.' Is this the kind of marriage you and Julia have?"

"We have a nice life together."

Had, not have.

Yes, we had a nice life together. In the midst of a battle royal, we'd catch each other's eye and unaccountably start to chuckle. And end up in bed. We weren't on our best behaviour like we are now, scared to make waves in the shipwreck of our lives.

"Julia," the therapist says, "Why so dramatic? Why so intense? Isn't there *anything* good about this guy?"

"He's got a great body and a full head of hair."

"Be serious, Julia. Make a list for next time. Tell me what you like about Rob. What's your best memory of him?"

The list:

    1. He's got a great body and a full head of hair. How many

men do I know who could fit into the jeans they wore in high school?

2. He's a wacky guy. At our reunion, that's what he wore. His torn jeans from Grade XI. And Jennie's leather jacket. There we were, me dressed to kill and Rob looking like the Fonz.

3. He's a wonderful father.

My best memory of you: the day we brought Tamara home from the hospital, the air stung with cold. When you came to fetch us, you couldn't park close by, and we had to walk a bit. I thought the baby was fine in the snowsuit, but I had no idea it was so cold. And so before we stepped outside, you unzipped your down jacket and placed her next to your heart.

"Rob, can you comment on Julia's list?" the therapist asks at the next session.

"Tamara's birth was the peak moment of my life."

I sneak a sideways glance at you. Your eyes are unnaturally bright. The therapist extends the box of tissues. We each take one.

You say to her, "I have never felt such ... *joy*. We took childbirth classes with both children. I hadn't expected to like them. It was a bit like coming here. Julia made me go to the first class and I got hooked. But with Jennie there were complications. I worked so hard with Julia, but the doctor wouldn't let me stay for the birth. For Tamara I was there. I can't tell you what that was like. One minute you're staring at this spot on the table and there's nothing. Well, not nothing. There's Julia, and she's magnificent, she's in control even though she's absolutely exhausted. But there's no baby yet. And the next minute there's the tip of Tamara's head and a tiny shock of black hair. It sounds corny, but it was a miracle."

The therapist nods. "It is a miracle."

She leans toward you. "Do you think Julia controls your life too much?"

"Julia's the best thing that's ever happened to me."

I keep thinking of the Barbie and Ken dolls and what they might have meant to you and Michelle. I keep thinking that, if our best memories of each other are from when Tamara was a baby, what's to keep us together now that she's turning thirteen. I keep thinking of my three nights in the hotel before you said you'd see the therapist and of how we sleep these days spoon style with your chin resting on my shoulder.

I keep asking myself what's the best thing that ever happened to me.

NORRIS DOMINGUE

Juana's Daughter

Sidney was talking. He was always talking.

"Now don't get me wrong! I like Mexico and the Mexicans, but, well, let me tell you about our housekeeper. Everyday, I give Juana some money to buy some food, and you know what she does?"

I hadn't the slightest idea.

It seems that Juana would manage to get the most inexpensive food, tell Sidney it cost more, and pocket the difference.

"And that daughter of hers is just as bad," added Edward.

Sidney and Edward had moved into San Miguel de Allende four months ago. I had been in Mexico about six weeks when I decided to spend the last week of it with them. We had known each other and worked together in theatre productions in Houston. Sidney was a dancer, and Edward was a set designer and artist.

The after dinner conversation, on the day of my arrival, was about Edward's latest canvas, the new plays back in the States, the economical viewpoint of the American tourist in Mexico, and the inadequacy of the Mexican servants.

The following morning, I was awakened for breakfast by Juana's daughter. The guys had failed to mention that she was a beauty. She was standing in the doorway with the sunlight behind her. She wore a brightly coloured blouse and a white skirt that you could see through. The long black hair, seemingly uncontrolled, made her golden skin appear even more so. Her dark eyes were smiling.

"Buenos dias," she said.

At first I was certain that one of us had the wrong room, 'til I heard the flapping footsteps of big, fat Juana in the hallway. I thanked this young beauty for waking me. She turned to walk away, and her movement was not of a peasant's daughter but more like that of a Mexican aristocrat.

How does an American approach a Mexican girl? In the midst of a mental procedure concerning this situation, I suddenly heard a baby crying. In the kitchen was a tiny dark skinned baby wrapped with a dirty rebozo lying in an old basket. My project of having this beauty alone was shot to hell when Juana told me that her daughter was the mother of the child.

After breakfast, I was entertaining the baby when Juana came running in to tell me that her daughter was ill. Sidney told me not to worry about it for there isn't anything to do when "these people" get sick. It comes from bad food, unclean food, or no food.

I thought I should at least try to help, so Juana watched the baby while I climbed up to the rooftop room where the girl was. She had gotten sick just outside the door; Juana – and the pan – had arrived too late.

I rushed into the brightly lighted room to see the young mother lying on a couch. She must have been in pain, yet she smiled.

Returning the smile, I asked, "Malo?"

She nodded. A tear rolled off her cheek as she smiled again.

I pointed just below her full breast to her stomach.

"Aqui?"

She nodded.

I had some pills that tourists are warned to take along in case of such attacks. I gave her two of them with some water. it was not long before she fell asleep.

When Sidney found out that I had tried to help, he thought me foolish.

"Besides, the girl's no good. The baby is a bastard. No-one

knows who the father is!"

The next morning I arose early and started a tour about the colourful village. The pink churches, the golden bells, the gray cobblestone streets, the green cactus plants, and the brown people were instrumental in my escape from the ever-present picture of Juana's daughter lying on that couch.

As I passed a large church near the plaza, a funeral procession was in progress. The small wooden cross followed by many white-clad altar boys, three priests, a black velvet coffin, and loved ones dressed in black – some without shoes – created a hallowed atmosphere. There were many people standing along the streets watching the funeral; the women made the sign of the cross, and the men removed their battered straw hats.

I glanced across the weather-beaten faces. Then I saw Juana's daughter. She was holding the baby, and the mother was standing behind her. Her long black hair fell slightly over one eye, and the cheap white dress clung to her well-formed body. I was ashamed of my thoughts as the coffin went by.

She caught me looking at her. She smiled.

With a sheepish grin, I waved and turned to walk away when I heard Juana call. She invited me to come see their home. I was delighted. Together we walked towards the outskirts of the village.

A sun-baked canal ran in front of their mud home, and, from the odour, I gathered it was really part of the town's sewer system. Almost every moving stream is. The four-room hut was surrounded by a high mud wall. The rooms were unheated and cold. Those thick walls keep out the sun's rays. For warmth, one had to step outside in the patio and, at night, sleep two to a bed.

Juana happily showed me pictures of the family, then she disappeared into the kitchen, leaving the daughter and me alone. When you don't know the language, it is not easy. Anyway, we mostly just sat and smiled. After a few minutes, she reached over to take my hand, a language I understood, and gently pulled me from the chair over to the bed. I couldn't help wondering if she wanted me to feel the material.

She pointed to herself, then to me and patted the bed.

"La noche. Comprende? "

I understood.

In poor Spanish, I asked what time tonight.

She told me that tonight there would be a fiesta in honour of the governor and, as at every fiesta, fireworks. We were to meet accidentally at the plaza, and later, when the fireworks began, we'd slip away. The entire village would watch the fireworks, including Juana.

The thing that strikes me funny now is that I really wanted to watch the fireworks, too. It's sort of making love and watching television.

All went as expected and we slipped away from the village. We made love in that cold hut ... without words; we spoke with our eyes, our hands, our bodies.

I never learned the girl's name. On the last morning, she came to say goodbye; no words again, only with the eyes. I gave her some earrings that I knew she liked. I gave the baby a toy. I handed Juana some money to cheer her. It was a sad occasion. We had grown fond of each other.

About four months later, I received a card from Sidney. The baby had died, but Juana's daughter was with child again. The card went on, "the girl's no good. No one knows who the father is."

J.G. Lewis

A Date with Lily

The Canadian sailor looked at his watch and at the sea of laughing Dubliners, their tables overflowing with pitchers of beer. He was sorry he had started drinking so early.

"What time did she say she'd be here?" he asked.

"Soon as she's free," said the brunette who was painting her fingernails with red polish.

The quiet girl with little pigeon eyes said nothing.

The sailor looked them over. He preferred sitting with them to sitting alone, he supposed, but Lily's friends weren't much for company. They certainly weren't dogs, but they didn't seem very bright. He had tried every one of his jokes, and he had still failed to amuse them.

"Jerry!" He heard his name called across the smoke-filled hall. He turned to see a couple of his buddies, his running-ashore mates. They were sitting with a group of Irish girls, including the nurse he had felt up in the taxi the night before he met Lily. The nurse was giving him the eye real good.

"I'll see you guys later," he shouted back to his buddies. His voice sounded loud and masculine. If only his tongue didn't feel so thick in his mouth.

A few minutes later he felt a hand on his shoulder. It was Tyler, his closest buddy.

"Come on over! She wants to talk to you!" his buddy shouted in his ear.

Just as the sailor began to stand up, the brunette fixed him with a stare.

"I thought you were going to wait for Lily," she said.

"I'll be right back," he told her.

"No, you won't. You're going off with that one over there."

"No, really," he grinned. "I was just going to talk to my friends."

"Sure," the brunette said.

He hated that look on her face. But he knew that, if he even glanced at the nurse, the brunette would tell Lily. The bitch. He hated sitting with these two. But he wanted so badly to see Lily again. He told Tyler to make some excuse for him. There was nothing he could do but drink to blot out the boredom.

The Canadian sailor ordered another round of beer for the table. He drained the remaining pitcher long before the serving girl arrived. She was all curves and hair. As she bent over him to deposit the pitchers on his table, her breasts hung right in front of his face. There was really no place else to look, but she was so close to him that he had to turn his head away.

By the time she stood erect he was ready with a Canadian twenty-dollar bill and a big smile.

"We'll pay for our own, thanks," the brunette said, reaching for her purse.

"My treat," he insisted and dropped his money on the serving girl's tray.

The brunette shrugged and shut her purse. She continued painting her fingernails. The pigeon-eyed girl said nothing.

With every passing second, boredom grew more heavily upon the sailor. Just as he was wondering how he could keep these girls amused, he was struck by inspiration.

"I want you to paint my nails," he told the brunette.

She looked at him for a moment, then said, "All right."

She took his right hand in her own and began applying the red liquid. This is something, he told himself, and grinned. Her touch was warm and comfortable. He wondered if she had a boyfriend.

"How long have you been in the navy?" she asked without missing a stroke.

"Three years." He had been a seaman for less than a year now, and this was the farthest he had ever been from home.

"And just what is it you do on that ship of yours?" she asked without looking up.

He was about to tell her he was a radar specialist, when he remembered that his red trade insignia was clearly visible on his uniform sleeve. The place was filled with too many Canadian seamen for him to risk such a lie.

"I'm a steward," he admitted.

"What's that?" the quiet girl said, setting her little pigeon eyes on him.

"Working in the wardroom, serving drinks and meals to the officers."

"Oh," said the brunette. "You're like a waiter."

"No, no." He fought to make himself heard over the din. "You have to know a lot. Really. How to mix drinks. The right wine for each meal. How to serve it."

"My brother's a waiter," the quiet one said.

"Sounds like a lot of drinking," the brunette said.

"Yeah," he admitted. "There's really not a lot to do on a ship when you're out at sea."

"At least not for the officers, it don't sound like," the brunette said. "Time for the other hand."

He raised his left hand and watched her go to work on it. She was right, he supposed. He really didn't like working with the officers. He had chosen his trade only because the training centre for stewards was in his home town. For a few months, he had seen his family as much as he wanted, and he had shown off his uniform to his friends. And now he was stuck with a trade he hated.

"I hope she gets here soon," he said.

"She has to look in on her dad," the brunette said.

"He's sick," the quiet one said. "Bad heart. Been laid up in bed for a month now."

He felt ashamed that he knew so little about Lily. They had barely exchanged more than a few words. He had spent most of the previous night kissing her and trying to feel her up. He wasn't sure that he wanted a girl with problems. He had enough of his own. An alcoholic stepfather. A mother who never had a thought about anything except playing bingo. And an older brother who got all the girls and beat him up every time they got together.

"There," the brunette said at last. "You're done."

The sailor looked at the ten red panes on his fingers. It was too silly for words. He didn't want Lily to see him looking like this. And he certainly didn't want his shipmates to see this. He would be a laughingstock for months.

"Okay," he said. "Let's take it off."

"What do you mean?" the brunette said. "I thought you liked it."

"Well, a joke's a joke," he said, "but now I want it off."

"I don't have anything to take it off," she said, looking at him without expression.

A few seconds passed before a set of emotions rippled through his drunken brain. He felt anger at first. He cursed the brunette, and he cursed his own stupidity. Then a calm settled over him. He almost laughed as he scratched and rubbed at the polish on his thumbnail. Bits of red paint fell over his navy uniform. At this rate it would take at least an hour to get the vile stuff off his hands. Even then he wouldn't be able to scrape it all off before Lily arrived. Of course she would notice it. The only thing he could do was tell her the truth.

Ken McDonough

Car Trouble

He kept his eyes on the highway ahead of him, like he had been taught when he was sixteen. He had learned to drive on the Prairies, where the flatness could dull your senses and cause accidents. Now that he was heading back from Vancouver to Montreal, he believed that his upbringing gave him a special advantage over the other drivers, the way an Irishman might fancy himself a superior drunk.

He felt odd. He had shaken his son's hand when he had become a new father (the boy had drawn him near, but his own hug was more like a stiff roundabout pat on the back); he had wept in the privacy of his car when his daughter had gotten married. It was the way he was made, he told himself. Why should it be any different this time round?

Because it was different. That's what the voice in his head kept hammering, the voice he tried to dislodge by switching radio stations and deliberately shifting focus. *Your sister died of cancer less than twenty-four hours ago, and you're heading home as if from Sunday dinner at your mother's. Did you see your mom's face?* He shrugged his shoulders irritably, as if to fend off a pestering friend. She was fine, he told himself. She knew he had to be back in Montreal on Friday; he had planned it that way. *Plans change.* No, they don't. Not for him. If he said he was going to do something, he did it; if he said he was going to be someplace by one fifteen, he was there at quarter past the hour. He had kept his commitment on this trip, too; nothing wrong there. *You even worked it all out on a piece of paper before leaving – time of departure, time of arrival, length of stay, the drive home – and recorded miles travelled and gas consumed after every fill-up ...* Well, nothing wrong with being dependable, either. *Like those camping trips in the middle of July...*

*rolled up the windows all the way, drove until noon, then out on the road
again until nightfall.*

The voice reminded him of his son, always squirming in the
back seat, reminding him how hot it was, clicking the button on
the rear door up and down to let him know he wanted to get out.
"What if I don't want to look around?" The sound of his own
voice surprised him. He scanned the road for other drivers, then
back at the pair of taillights directly ahead of him. "What if I like
the feel of the car moving down the highway? What if I like to see
the number of miles fall away until I get to a place? If that's where
I get my satisfaction, is it a crime?" *No, but what about the captive
audience you're dragging around with you? What about the tone in
your mother's voice when you told her you were driving out?* "What
tone?" *The one she got that says your sister's on her deathbed and
wants to talk to you and you're taking the car from Montreal to
Vancouver!*

He reached again for the radio, turning the volume up. His
sister had died two days before he had arrived. He knew the airlines
kept seats aside for family emergencies. Hell, everybody knew that
– he suspected his mother did, too – but he had decided to drive
out anyway. He could even remember the struggle in his head as
he reasoned that there would be no seats available on such short
notice and that if he drove straight across the country, stopping
only for sleep and a meal, he'd hit Vancouver in four, five days
tops. *You were conscious of tricking yourself.* "You already know
that!" he shot back. Hell, the guilt over the lie he would tell his
mother had nagged him all the way across the Prairies and through
the mountains. It's just that … it wasn't supposed to happen.
Things didn't get lost. More importantly, *people* didn't get lost.
Every workday he had gotten up at six in the morning, had eaten
the orange and the bowl of oatmeal his wife had set out for him
the previous night, and had left at precisely six forty. He had never
once been ill in twenty-five years, never lost anything or anyone.

All possessions and people had been accounted for right up to the day he would pass away himself, which, if he was the statistical average (and he hoped he was), wouldn't be for another twenty-five years. *You think rituals stop time?* "Never said that." *Didn't have to. Never got sick as long as an orange and a bowl of oatmeal were waiting for you everyday, in the exact same spot, at the exact same time. You're like a superstitious baseball player who spits tobacco over his shoulder or walks backward into the dugout before every game, thinking it'll save him from a losing streak. Thought you had outfoxed what had fooled everyone else ...*

He once again fiddled with the radio, knew he wouldn't find what he was looking for, and finally shut if off. The car swerved ever so slightly, sending a prickling sensation through his body. Maybe he should have left the road, but he had no time to stop; he was expected in Montreal before supper on Friday. He had told his wife, so there was no getting around it. He adjusted his seat and concentrated on the road.

The voice was right. Did he really believe that driving there would slow his sister's cancer, maybe halt it altogether? He wasn't sure. Perhaps it was denial; when he arrived he would find her running to the door with a big grin on her face – "April Fool's!" Or maybe he just couldn't handle the idea of being there when her eyes closed one last time, his name still on her lips. "Is that it?" No voice answered this time, just the regular thrum of traffic that had held him safe for most of his adult life.

"I couldn't make it ... I'm sorry ... I drove as fast as I could." He heard the words falling from his mouth and knew it was just an excuse. He imagined she did, too. Even as the thought surfaced, he could feel the tears crawling painfully up his chest like slow mercury through a thermometer. They would come sooner or later. Already the cars up ahead were blurring. They would come, and he would have to find a place off the road, far from the passing traffic. His car swerved again as he stumbled home as best he could.

SUSAN MOTYKA

The Dictionary

She was not loaded down with bags, as were some of the other passengers. Eva watched the men and women as they headed toward the ship, carrying suitcases and holding bundles that sagged with the weight of their contents. Eva had only one small suitcase, made of pressed cardboard, and was secretly proud of its lightness and portability. She was fifteen, about to join her cousin Maria in the new country, and did not need to take much beyond her papers and some clothes. She was young, still not weighted down with things that held memories or meaning.

She and Aunt Dorota walked to the dock. They were close to the sea yet could not smell it: a brisk wind coming off the land swept away all scent, blowing particles of dust through Eva's long, oak-coloured braids and into the folds of her white blouse. As they neared the embarkation line, Aunt Dorota suddenly stopped. She was a tall woman with dove-grey eyes half-hidden by lids that drooped, as though she could not bear to take in the world fully any longer. She was Eva's mother's older sister and had raised Eva after both of the girl's parents died in the influenza epidemic of 1918, when Eva was a young child.

Almost shyly, Aunt Dorota handed Eva a small, heavy package wrapped in brown paper. Eva undid the neat folds of paper to reveal a slightly tattered English dictionary, covered in dark-blue cloth.

Aunt Dorota smiled. "Remember, it's not a real dictionary until you press in it the flowers given to you by some young, handsome man." She hugged Eva tightly, pointed her chin in the direction of the embarkation line, turned, and quickly walked away.

After the first evening, in which they sailed into a sunset that looked as though it would swallow the ship, Eva settled into a routine. She carried her dictionary everywhere, cradling it like an armful of the delicate first potatoes of spring. She practiced moving her mouth through the obstacle course of consonants and vowels. Eva had been a schoolgirl the week before; it was comforting to study the dictionary, to feel some small link with the place she had left. With each word memorized, she felt the dictionary provided a way into the new country, a means of turning the new country into a home. She also watched the handsome officers, with their waxed, mahogany-coloured mustaches, moving about the ship. She closed her eyes and imagined dancing in the arms of one of the officers: being guided over the dance floor as firmly yet gently as the ship, which moved smoothly through the North Sea and then the Atlantic. She dreamed about such a man one day handing her a fragrant bouquet, whose petals would perfume the dictionary.

Eva continued to study her dictionary on the train between Halifax and Montreal, and forever after the memory of learning the new language would be entwined with the sensation of being rocked from side to side: first the soft, lullaby-like rhythm of the ship and then the sharper, metallic jolts of the rails.

Eva moved into the small apartment in Montreal that housed her cousin Maria, Maria's husband, and their four children. Maria found Eva a job at a factory, sewing buttons onto men's coats for a few cents a week. Because she navigated English better than many of the other women at the factory, Eva was asked to help those whose mother tongue was Italian, or Hungarian, or Portuguese, with letters to be written in English. At first Eva felt that she could not take the coins that were put into her hand for this work, but slowly she realized that they represented a way of saying "thank you" outside of language. The words of thanks were stronger, were more complete, it seemed to Eva, when accompanied by a few pieces of copper or silver. With the coins she was given Eva bought magazines, which she and the other women looked through on their lunch breaks. They would open the magazines on the large table at which they sat and take turns reading aloud, their voices becoming more confident at navigating the new language.

While the other women read from the magazines, Eva studied the advertisements. She was drawn to the poised and serene women on the glossy pages. They glided silently through a life of beauty. She imagined the ship's officers lining up to dance with women such as these. She examined the women closely, noting the details of their appearance. She would close her eyes and picture herself among them, waiting for a dance partner.

After a few months at the factory, Eva was approached by a woman with whom she worked. The woman's husband was a marriage broker and seeking a woman of Eva's background to introduce to a client. Would Eva be interested? Eva considered for a moment and told the woman that in her country it was customary for the man to make a payment to the bride's family. She held her breath as the woman hesitated before replying that this would be possible.

That evening, Eva dressed in her best clothes. In front of the one tiny mirror in the apartment, she cut off her braids with Maria's sewing scissors so that she more closely resembled the women in the magazine advertisements. Eva's chin-length hair would remind all those who saw her that she was now a woman of this country, a woman who had come here not to start over but to begin.

Eva walked to the broker's apartment and was admitted to a small living room. The broker, an old man, sat on a sofa beside a younger, sandy-haired man with two diagonal creases on his forehead, like an arrow pointing to the space between his eyes. The way in which he watched Eva reminded her of the men who assessed the animals at her uncle's horse farm. Yet he did not seem unkind.

"Young, strong," the young man said, nodding.

His voice, deep and even, pleased Eva; if she closed her eyes, the voice could belong to one of the officers on the ship.

She took a lock of short hair between her fingers and held it forward for the men to see. "Shiny," she said. "Healthy."

The men walked to the kitchen to confer in low voices. The old man returned and stated an amount that seemed low to Eva. He pointed to the area where her long braids had hung and explained, "Your hair is missing."

"I speak, read, and write English," Eva said. "That will raise the price."

Back at the apartment she had shared with Maria and the others, Eva pulled out her suitcase and dictionary and packed her few clothes. She pulled out from behind the waistband of her skirt the roll of bills that the marriage broker had handed her. She and Edward, the young man, would be married the following day. Eva separated a few bills from the roll: those would go to Maria, for all that she had provided Eva. Eva ran a hand under the soft new edge of her hair. One day, she thought, I will be one of the women with whom the ship's officers would dance. Until then, I will need help, and I must be able to thank people properly. Eva then put the remainder of the money between two pages of her dictionary and closed it, pressing down firmly.

Cambodian Rock Song No. 4

I asked where the cows were, and everybody looked at me as though I were crazy. Then I asked where they kept the meat, and Delvecchio the foreman pointed over to the vats. Vats was the wrong word, they were like little railroad cars you would see in a television show about Victorian-era coal mines, rumbling through the tunnels, full of hypnotized black-faced children. The vats *did* have meat in them, liquefied and waiting to be shot into moulds of pimento loaf or more imaginative casings. It was my job, my new job, to circulate through the plant, scoop up the liquid meat in little baggies, and perform a fat-content analysis on each sample.

It was not a happy time to be working at the plant. There were no cows at the packing house because the operation was in the process of being gradually shut down; with the killing floor idled they now only processed and packaged meats shipped in from other plants. Layoffs had gutted two full shifts and those still employed had a resigned look, that gaunt end-of-the-siege stare. When I showed up at that summer job, fresh from university finals, I was met with a seething contempt, immediate and communal. Had I been a baseball bat-wielding Pinkerton, I could not have produced a more complete solidarity among the other workers.

I was made part of a quality-assurance team, three guys who patrolled the plant measuring effluent E. coli and mouse droppings in parts-per-million and who revelled in the fact that they chose to include me in their group despite the fact that I was hated, even by them. They set themselves apart, commandeering a separate table in the cafeteria, where I was given a chair and dealt a hand in some inane lunch-hour card game that I played with a disinterest that further estranged me from my tablemates, Ed and Steve and Gordie. They argued about sports. None of them ever talked about having any other job before the plant. I imagined that they were like many and had applied right after high school. On the second day, Ed asked me what I had studied, and I told him about an introductory physics course I had taken, about how it was centripetal and not centrifugal force, and I explained entropy to his blank, then smirking, face. The others seemed to find the laws of thermodynamics hilarious as well. By day three I was calculating minutes: end of the shift, end of the week, end of the job. I finished every workday by making the journey between the rows of margarine-rendering tanks to my laboratory, slouching to avoid the oily mist that hung in the air and that shrouded the huge metal sentinels, my coat pockets full of liquid meat in doggie bags, my lungs inhaling atomized animals. I hated my job and my co-workers. I shouted fantastic obscenities made inaudible by the machine-roar. I cursed my more well-off friends who spent their summers travelling in Europe and was prone to dark, elaborate thoughts concerning their journeys: malaria was contracted, cathedrals collapsed, planes disappeared from radar screens. My wrath was limitless, my relief fleeting.

It was in my windowless laboratory – where I daily perfected the art of adding sulphuric acid to the meat slurry in order to accurately measure fat content – that I first heard Cambodian Rock Song No.4. *You have to hear this*, a friend said, handing over a worn cassette as we drank beer in his basement the night before. He had just returned from Asia and had about him an easy glow of road wisdom and sexual satiety, that well-recognized traveller's patina that I wanted to take a blow-torch to but instead had to satisfy myself by accepting his tape. I put the cassette in my walkman. If nothing else, his kind gift (which I had already calculated how far I could throw) would be a diversion, and I needed diversion.

I listened. I was hooked. The Cambodian Rock Songs were anonymously performed and untitled except for their numbers – 1 through 14 – which made them seem even more exotic, like new elements, glowing and dense, added to the end of the periodic table. The master tapes had allegedly banged around southeast Asia, surviving napalm and Pol Pot, before dropping into the hands of those like my travelling friend's.

I listened to it at work, especially Cambodian Rock Song No. 4. It was my solace. At first I thought it may have been more the noise than music, the diversion of soft sponge headphones against my ears and the movement of the tape. But I was wrong: it was something about the song. It opened with jangly, almost inadvertent guitar chords, followed by an organ wheezing in accompaniment; then came the voices, heard in the background, not singing but talking in barely audible, conspiratorial Cambodian chitchat, as though fretting whether the Khmer Rouge was going to break down the door for some fresh skulls. I wasn't angry after that. I don't know why. It could have been a neurochemical thing, something to do with serotonin. Maybe I was getting mellow with the toxic effects of inhaling too much vaporized pork, but, whatever the reason, it became easier for me. I went to work every day in that huge empty shell of a packing house, listened to music, measured the fat, and learned to play poker. The plant itself still frightened me, but it had become beautiful too. It was an awesome place in the evening, emptied like a carcass, a huge thorax ribbed by ventilation shafts. I would look at it and could only think of the second law of thermo-dynamics, the movement of energy; that everything was breaking down and emptying out, and that we could only temporarily forestall it, reassembling ourselves until we began to fall apart again.

By August they had announced more firings at the plant. People no longer played cards at lunch, but sat in silence, chewing and mentally dividing their severance pay by their monthly expenditures. Ed, who I had been told drank too much, showed up at work with plum-coloured bruises under each eye. There was talk of a two-four, a car, and a tree. Now he took the bus to work. Steve said nothing, but Gordie laughed and told him he looked like a raccoon. Ed reached across the table, and soon the two were on the floor, sprawling among upturned chairs and horrified, expectant onlookers.

Driving home that day, I saw Ed at the bus stop. He tried for a moment not to make eye contact, but I was intent on giving him a ride, and he finally accepted. He told me where he lived, and, when I said I knew the neighbourhood, he seemed surprised.

I wanted to play the tape for Ed, to have Cambodian Rock Song No. 4 kick in like an antidote, an auditory ipecac, slapping him on the back like it did for me. I wanted it to wake him up, to let him know that somewhere, somebody had been disobeying the second law, creating something from nothing, telling the powers that be that they would have to wait to polish his skull, as there was music to make. I rummaged around the scattering of cassettes on the little shelf under the dashboard before remembering that I had left the tape at work. Ed and I rode home without a word between us, listening to the radio instead.

Distances

D. Beloved, I once might have said, but that was some time ago. Now, only your absence weighs upon this place, this small expanse of crystallized time and captured existences. I'm not talking to you tonight, but to the space inside myself that is you. If it mattered, I'd tell you that I'm sitting in our room of shadows, that the bed sheets are as we once would have left them, twisted like dampened towels after they've been wrung out. The wallpaper is still peeling off in tiny flakes, gray-like shavings of bark stripped from an old tree. Outside our window, clouds of colour roll across the surface of the lake. The cormorants have congregated eagerly on the rocky shoreline, their strange heads cocked slightly and their feathers tucked neatly away.

And she stands among them, our Colby, her back to the window, to me, her bundle of hair flying in the wind. She's looking out over the lake. She's too close, it seems, to the water. How she's drawn to it, like the birds, yearning for some sort of liberation.

She was always a quiet child. Her hands were so expressive; her fingers gracefully long. Gradually, I have watched her become more like you each day. There's no laughter in this house, only signs of comings and goings – shoes tossed carelessly onto the doormat, keys left sitting on the dining room table, telephone calls from people I've never met. It's as though she isn't really here at all, as though we're living in two parallel dimensions that happen, by chance, to overlap every now and then. She does everything with such detachment. I reach for her and want to hold her, but I can't. And I feel them again, those moments that I associate so closely with you. Moments like sand escaping though the spaces between my fingers even when I make a fist.

The sacred birds are all around her. How different they are from the mad ducks who flap wildly about, pecking at the earth for scraps of food. These birds are silent, utterly still. They look almost pious, as though they're gathered in prayer. But what is it that they worship? The sweeping waters, the infinite sky? I don't know, D. I know that the night is more immense than it has ever seemed. And, in your world, where the street lamps of the city dampen the glow of the pinpricks of light above, it is starless. Loveless. Without God.

I remember a time when I was younger, here in this place, before the sickness defeated my father, when his lungs still filled easily with air. He was a stern, distant man in those days. If he spoke to me at all, it was either harshly or apathetically. He kept his distance, and I believe, now, that only the lake allowed us to develop any kind of connection, a bond that he wouldn't otherwise have been able to make. As we moved slowly through the water in his old skiff, his arms would swell with the effort of thrusting the pole deep into the murky depths. Looking into the water, I sometimes thought that I could see the flash of scales on the slimy backs of gliding trout. Trailing my fingers in the water, I thought that I could touch them.

One day, we were in the boat, resting on the far side of the lake, a marshy area where giant lily pads sprouted up from out of the water. He was cursing the gnats that swarmed in clouds over the monstrous flowers, so large that they appeared to have over-bloomed, stretched out of their intended proportions. He saw it first, rising from out of the green stalks. The cormorant climbing sacredly into the warm air, stretching its wings out and lifting upwards. We stood there on the boat, captured together, in awe of the sureness of the flight. Oh, but that was long ago, long before you became a part of the lake, of this room and its shadows.

Do you remember when you first came to this house, and we sat outside, in the backyard? No-one had bothered to move the boat when he died. It sat, overturned, on the lawn, and you walked over and pounded on it with your strong fist, laughing. "What's this old heap of rubbish?" you asked. And then you hoisted yourself up onto it and lit a cigarette. After you were finished, you tossed the butt, still smoldering, and it rolled onto the metal and came to rest. I didn't think about it until much later, when we were lying next to each other in the darkness, in the half-moon shadows, damp and breathing. I turned to you to impart ... what was it? My secrets, my silent dreams, the aimless stories of birds? God, I knew I spoke of trivial things that wouldn't ever be remembered. But I had a need. A need to be heard. A need for compassion. Most of all, for love. And you could only bury your face in the pillow, nodding impatiently. Finally, you rolled over and pulled the blankets around you. "Go to sleep, love," you said. Love, you called me, as though you gave a damn. And in the lightlessness, I thought of my father. I thought of his old boat resting sorrowfully in the muck, in the weed tangle, abandoned. And all I could see in my mind was you, so carelessly tossing away your cigarette, the tip still glowing.

As time brought us together, I began to notice, more and more, your strange distance from the world, from people. Sometimes, sitting across from you a restaurant, I saw your eyes glaze over. You'd start to tap your fingers impatiently on the table, staring blankly beyond me, into the distance. When I asked you about it later, you just shrugged it off, as though you didn't know what I meant or remember what I was talking about.

I don't know when it was that I began to think often of the cormorants. In some strange way, I longed for them, for their whole and unbroken union with the lake and the open space above. There was a perfect oneness between bird and water, bird and sky, and I ached for such a unity. Every time I reached for you, I became more conscious of the width between us, the certainty of your indifference. I knew it wasn't calculated, and that was the worst part. It was not something of your own design, something that could be changed, a barrier to be broken though. It existed a your core. And maybe that's what has destroyed me all of these years. I love a man who will never understand the softness of being, the spaces, opened in the dark burrows of night, where hands and voices must meet.

D., I dreamt of you last night. In my dream, you turned to me. You cried. And I can hear the echoes of those tears now, those tears never shed, as I watch our daughter from the window, encompassed in her own wilderness, in her own silence. And what I would like is to lie down in the shadows and shabbiness of this room, to wrap myself in the sheets and feel you breathing next to me, as though this one sacred moment is all the deliverance either one of us will ever need. Most of all, I would like you to turn to me and whisper.

2001-2002

Sarah Venart

What got her single and sad? Jesus. Does Mr. Marco think *that's* a good place to start, impression-wise?

What got her *sad*? Hell, *sadness* got her sad, enough said. As for what got her single, that's private, really. Doesn't he think? And *why* does he want to know what her religion is, anyway? That's weird. Does she need to remind him that this thing they've started is *not* a budding question-and-answer period; this is a correspondence. But, okay. If she has a religion, it is that she hopes in the face of heartache. She hopes in the window of an apartment that catches the geared-down sounds of intersection traffic, highlighted by the occasional yawp of a dog attempting the impossible cross.

Does that answer the question, Mr. Marco? Is that a religion?

Now, one more thing: she bets Mr. Marco has a great accent, being from New York. She loves the way New Yorkers talk and how the streets there smell like dirty skin and decayed wool, in a nice way. Coming into the city in a cab, she likes how the skyline of buildings goes and goes and goes. Does Mr Marco like that too?

Mr. Marco appears to believe that love is a verb. Is that it? Is that why he writes to her every day? His earnestness is sweet. And she apologizes – she's sorry for saying Mr. Marco's from Brooklyn, he's *from* Vermont, actually. (A place she imagines as permanently green, a verdant Oz with hippies instead of midgets and witches. But she doubts that that is a fair description.)

One more thing. She thought his last name was Marco, but no. It is Spiel. So it is Marco Spiel. What sort of a last name is that? She likes it okay. It sounds like a square dance move: *Spiel yer partner round the floor, now do-si-do and do it some more.* It sounds like fun and games. It reminds her of one night when she was drunk and passed out on the couch and her ex-boyfriend – she'll call him Ex – came to carry her off to bed. When he picked her up, she said, quite out of the blue, "Show me on the doll where you'll touch me." She doesn't know where it came from, that line, probably a movie she'd seen or a television show. She liked the sound of it and thought it was funny, but it freaked Ex out rather badly. He didn't think it was funny. He said the reason he had to slap her was to wake her, but she knew that he was really just horrified by her candour.

Not yet, Mr. Marco. No, she can't meet him, but it is lovely to be insisted upon. Courtship makes anyone feel pretty, and she's no different. She likes the whole tackling and insisted-uponness of chivalry. She could do Vermont in a month or two. Maybe. His description of the hotel they should meet at, the one atop the mountain, sounds a little like the hotel in *Hotel New Hampshire*; but unlike that metaphor-filled home, his hotel sounds quite peaceful – no lesbians dressed in bear suits, no overly close sibling relationships. But tell her more about that hotel, about Vermont. It sounds so *uncity*.

Okay. She can do that. Since he liked the first story, the doll story, she'll tell another. Once, Ex woke her up one morning with the sweetest wake-up device. She won't explain the euphemism; she's sure Mr. Marco gets it. Ex was crawling up from the bottom of the bed and, well, he was doing ... stuff. Ex thought she was asleep, but in truth she was awake and felt like playing.

She mumbled, "No, Daddy, no." She expected him to get the humour and play back. Maybe say something like, "Daddy don't play that" and laugh. Or take her roughly. Or at least kiss her. Instead, Ex froze. Apparently, she had killed the moment, had made him pull on his jeans and leave the apartment for the honking traffic outside.

Well, Mr. Marco, to tell the truth, Ex was rarely impressed. Of course they fought. That's why he's Ex, right? They fought gracefully in the well-worn ring their kitchen table became. Like a cocky wrestler with too-smooth moves, Ex understood where she was going before she went. Towards the end, this bored her and she started avoiding home. She pretended instead that she had appointments and went to the cinema for the evening to write in the dark. She wrote in the dark when she watched movies.

So how is New York? She was there a week after the terrorist attacks to do some research. She shouldn't have gone; some part of her wasn't thinking. Of course it wasn't *at all* okay. She was writing this piece on lost people and places in cities, on the places and the people that city councils lose or forget about. She was planning to go to Coney Island; she had it in her mind that she would find something there to write about. But when she got to New York, in the cab from the airport, she saw American flag after American flag dipping crazily on the back of every bumper on the bumper-to-bumper freeway to Brooklyn. And yes, the skyline of buildings went on and on, but the air was acrid with smoke and the skyline had an unspeakable hack job at its centre. She forgot Coney Island – she could barely get her head around the faces of the people in Brooklyn. She couldn't begin to think about lost places because she saw them everywhere. She found herself sort of numbly walking around Brooklyn and watching people. She felt like *she* was missing something and everyone she passed on the street was broken and looking into each face on the street for the answer to that brokenness. Every movement was gentle or something – she doesn't know how to describe it, but Mr. Marco might know what she means.

And she's still feeling a little lost. Last night, she biked over to this old people's home. At five on the nose, they shuffle and walker and wheel into the cafeteria and fill table upon table with bodies in nighties and terry cloth robes. They eat their mashed potatoes and watery soups and Jell-O. It isn't sad, it's sobering. She likes to be sobered. The old people are eating, bent over their trays with their canes leaning against the tables or their walkers waiting beside them like stoic pets. She loves the way the room sort of vibrates: she means that way that the fluorescent lights kind of make the mint walls snap. She knows it might sound sad, but it *isn't*. It really isn't.

No, Mr. Marco. He misunderstood. She doesn't volunteer. She watches them from the window. She *should* volunteer. She knows that. She will soon, but she's busy these days. Anyway, she has another story for him. Last night, downtown, she found two places she'd like to show him, if they ever meet. First, this elderly concierge came out of his lobby like he was looking for her and he called her over. He said, See some birds, *Mademoiselle.*

She was grateful for the *Mademoiselle* and went inside. He pointed a finger at the lobby's ceiling like he was showing off a pharaoh's tomb.

Hundreds of tiny little sparrows carved into the brass vents.

Oh my, she said.

But the concierge was saving the real prize. His sweet little *Mademoiselle* and the birds in the brass were nothing compared to when he took her by the elbow and showed her an alley out back. It was really something she can't describe with words. She'd like to show Mr. Marco instead. So, if he comes to visit, if he sticks with her, if he picks his way through the trash and boxes and doesn't get upset about smells and refuse, if he actually makes it to the back of the alley, then she can show him how, with the right stranger, under that rusted staircase, if he cranes his neck up at this certain angle, the sky proves worthy.

How the night is suddenly exemplary.

Now she has to go. She wishes Mr. Marco his own cool and dark and sweet evening. He should go to a park. He should have an ice cream. He should look in the windows of apartments and retirement homes and report back on what he sees. She'd like that. The real kick is that *everywhere*, and in the oddest places, things are just waiting to present themselves. This thought is what stops her from feeling sad and single these days. She doesn't mind telling Mr. Marco that now. She knows him better, after all.

ENCONIUM

Matthew Anderson

Everyone's life can be reduced to a theme. Virgil knows it, with the same certainty he knows the streets headed north out of the city will be jammed on Friday afternoons, or that you shouldn't order fish in a restaurant on Mondays, or that the name he inherited from his maternal grandfather marked him as forever different and probably contributed to his eventual choice of career. Everyone's life, at least viewed in retrospect, has a motif. This is not some seminary learning – although God knows he could have used it as a younger cleric. It is an art gained through trial and error at a hundred awkward wakes. All he needs do is ask the right question about the deceased, and something the family will tell him, some detail half-forgotten, will awaken the voice in his head that says: "There. Focus on that. Use that."

He imagines himself a nobler cousin to the streetside caricaturists who deliver a sketch for ten dollars on Sunday afternoons at the port. Like them, he discovers the one characteristic that can bear exaggeration, that somehow contains the whole within the particular.

It is rarely the thing that the families themselves first offer up. Most children lack imagination about their parents, he realizes, and the headlong rush of so many to familial hagiography blinds them even further. Meta, for instance, was introduced by her grown son the stockbroker in much the same way Virgil had received a hundred lives: "She was a good person. Great mother. Loved her children and her grandchildren. She'd give you the shirt off her back if you needed it."

It was, if people only knew, a dulling litany of empty praise. At such times Virgil hoped his professionalism covered a rather unprofessional testiness. Was it that they didn't care enough to see their mother as a real human being, that they were too self-obsessed in their own loss to exercise some imagination and memory, or that they simply did not have the faculty for noticing the person they were pretending to honour? "A great neighbour." It was stifling to hear such phrases pasted up like boring adver-tising. Nothing remarkable at all. Everyone dies a saint.

Only after an hour of patient, slow sifting did Meta's daughter-in-law (they're often the sharpest eyes) say: "And don't forget about her singing."

"Singing?" Virgil repeated it as a question.

"Oh yes," said the son, already moving on to the next platitude.

"No, please," insisted Virgil. "Tell me about the singing."

"She was some kind of singer in Berlin before the war broke out."

"What kind of songs?"

Lieder, mostly. I think. Emma, what was it Oma used to sing in the cafés? Strauss ... was it Strauss? She would sing them to us as we were growing up too. Yeah, I remember, especially when we were sick. When we got older we got embarrassed or she did or something, I guess, because she never did it anymore."

Like an angler, Virgil kept bringing them back to that one trait: yes, she did sing, had hoped to professionally, gave it up to emigrate to Canada, still sang with the opera on the radio Saturday afternoons while she canned pickles and her husband Willi worked outside in the garden. The children had almost forgotten – maybe she had even forgotten – but he would not. His notes, upon returning home to his computer, had that one word underlined three times with several asterisks: singer. That was the hook on which to hang her memorial.

The Greeks knew how to give a good speech when someone died. None of this haphazard mewling at the microphone for them. As a student Virgil had heard his professor in Classics give the technical term, even then taking care to remember it: *encomium*. Starting with birth, you list the education, the virtues, the manner of life, the deeds, the achievements, and the honours bestowed. He was not so rigorous, perhaps. But he worked doggedly to glean some characteristic theme, and once in hand, it was remarkably easy to open the door into a stranger's life. Inevitably the families were surprised. "How could you know our mother so well?" Virgil would nod his thanks, embarrassed. They didn't see the template. How could he tell them how little it took, how little he still knew?

When he bothers to reflect on it he has trouble, now, distinguishing the stories of all the people he has buried, a lack of memory that leaves him slightly uneasy. A friend of his, a DJ with whom he likes to share off-colour jokes, once confided the difficulty of being everyone's best friend at the wedding reception, and how hard it is to keep couples straight when they are encountered later. He has a similar problem. His attention wanes faster than people might think.

It is a Friday afternoon. They will be stuck in traffic a good forty-five minutes before arriving at the cemetery. Sitting in the limousine with the casket, Virgil thinks: the poor finally ride like the rich – when it's to their funeral. He looks out the glass of the limo, seeing only his reflection. The problem with most eulogies is guilt. Trying not to miss anything, we say too much, and therefore nothing. The procession crawls the cross-lined hills. Finally Virgil leads the casket to the graveside. Takes his place.

"Dear friends, this is the story of a singer," he begins. His mind, however, is not on Meta, but her husband, standing lost there. So often lifelong partners die within months of each other. He was raised on a farm. What else? Tinkered with cars. Virgil wonders if he will remember this thought when it comes time to bury Willi. He'll make a note, file it. Fixing is an act of redemption, a strong Biblical image.

There is an angle to every life. This man's gardening is a paean to resurrection, that woman's international travel career leads straight to heavenly rest. Of course – how could it be otherwise? A Scottish dancer or a cowboy – now, those would be interesting but hardly insurmountable metaphorical problems. Virgil knows the temptation to triteness but pushes the line resolutely. Only when he is alone with the funeral home cheque in his pocket do the doubts sometimes rise up to trouble him.

"Sing a new song unto the Lord. This is the story of a life on an unexpected stage, and the song sung by love." When Virgil steps back momentarily from his eulogy, he surprises the mourners no less than himself by toppling into an open grave left carelessly unprotected. He hits the soft earth at full length. It knocks the air right out of him, so that for the briefest of moments he is unable to breathe. In that instant he lays wondering if this is what death feels like, if this is the final mansion to which so often he has been tour guide.

He wants to call, but no words come out. He is looking up at the blue, blue sky as at a distant window, the cold earth at his back. Feeling everything and nothing at once: the too-optimistic plastic green of the outdoor carpet dangling above, the drooping lilies calling him back up, the damp smell, his own unusual calmness. Where is the theme, the one characteristic they will use to unlock his life? The stockbroker peers over, a would-be rescuer. Virgil watches as clumps of earth, dislodged by the man's careless feet, fall like so many words over his astonished eyes.

Kirsty Robertson

Charlene sat down at the dinner table today and announced that she was going to be an art historian. Not that it was a big shock – she'd been weaving through the house all week, pretending she was on the Antiques Road Show, running her finger over the dining room table Mom and Dad had bought off the back of some truck. I'm sure this is worth something, she would say, tapping her finger on her teeth and smoothing her sleek hair behind her ear. She announced it on meatloaf night, as she sat down, picking at the dry crust of meat and trying to look worldly and intelligent.

Charlene never eats. She lives on coffee, cigarettes that she sneaks out of Mom's purse, and pastries from the Tim Horton's on the corner. Not doughnuts, only pastries – they're more sophisticated. But she's picking at her meatloaf and the tension in the room is growing. Charlene knows that Mom thinks she can't afford to go to university because her marks aren't good enough to get a scholarship. Charlene makes the announcement knowing Mom can't say anything about money. Mom spent the extra on a pair of pumps that are sitting in the hallway under the mirror.

Charlene saw them on her way to the dining room. I saw her notice. I had this whole speech in my head about how Mom deserves new shoes, but Charlene didn't say anything. Didn't even complain that we have to eat meatloaf because Mrs. Grover sent us a freezerload full when Dad passed on. That's what she said – "I've made you a freezer full of meatloaf Cheryl, because I know how hard it can be when your husband passes on." Like he'd been caught in the giant intestine of life or something. He had a heart attack mowing the lawn, and I watched the scorching red of his face fade to pale before the ambulance arrived. "All those girls," said Mrs. Grover. "All those girls."

Charlene knows everything there is to know about student loans. She went to the bank and the government office and the school counsellor and came home and dumped everything on the dining room table for Mom to look at. Mom wasn't home yet, and Charlene started bitching to me about how you couldn't get anywhere these days without a university degree. Everyone else managed to find the money, she said, so why couldn't we. Even Mrs. Grover's two sons had degrees from the Community College, and she knew she was smart enough to do well. She had pulled her grades up last semester. By the time she stopped to breathe Mom had come home and saw me and Charlene sitting at the table behind a foot-high stack of writing. She didn't even look at us before she kicked the new pumps down the hallway, complaining that her corns were killing her. "If you don't get me some coffee you'll be next," she said. Joking. Charlene jumped up and went into the kitchen strutting her art history walk and wearing her art history skirt, always believing that if you dress the part you become the person. So now she's walking around like some anorexic Antiques Road Show character in her little black skirt and V-neck sweater and her perfect hair and horn-rimmed glasses from Claire's Accessories. But Mom wants Charlene to go to university – you can tell by how agitated she gets whenever the subject comes up; she'll pinch the skin at the bridge of her nose or kick her pumps down the hall or something.

Then Mom asks where Jenny is, as if she doesn't know. Jenny's the youngest, she rarely comes out of her room and thrives on being a petulant thirteen-year-old über-teen. Mrs Grover gave her some kilt she'd dug up at a church bazaar somewhere, because "all the girls were wearing them" and she didn't want Jenny to start school without a new wardrobe. Jenny threw a fit because the kilt came two inches below her knee, and all the girls were wearing skirts that left their underwear showing and thigh-high stockings that made them look like half-pint whores. Mom made Jenny wear it anyway, because we had to pass Mrs. Grover's house on the way to school, and "she's been so kind after all." Halfway through the day, the kilt got a foot hacked off the bottom and was covered in duct tape and paint in art class until it stuck out like a silver tutu. And Mrs. Grover came over later to tell Mom that she'd seen Jenny walking by the house wearing some creation, and she wondered if she was in a play. Mom had to pull her best newly bereaved look to get her to leave. Jenny was told not to wear the kilt again, but she wears it all the time.

I'm picking at a scab on my elbow because I don't feel like telling Mom where Jenny is, and I'm sick of Charlene and her art history dreams. I know she's standing by the stove imagining that some hot young law student is going to walk by the art history department and fall immediately in love with her so that she can escape the kitchen linoleum that she hates so much. She'll bring him home to dinner so that we can parade before him like a freak show, and afterwards she'll give a little wave of her hand, and laugh sardonically and say "can you believe I came from this?" And then he'll laugh equally sardonically, and they'll head off into a distant future minus meatloaf and corns. Or something like that.

Charlene comes out of the kitchen carrying a cup of coffee, and the window is open so we can hear Mrs. Grover next door yelling for her cat Humphrey to come in. She's standing on the back porch with her hands on her hips screaming, "Here pussy! Pussy! Pussy!" so that everyone in the neighbourhood can hear her. And Charlene rolls her eyes and says "doesn't she know her boys are in the city?" just to get a rise out of Mom, but Mom starts snorting, and trying to smile and frown and the same time. Then all of a sudden she starts howling with laughter at the idea of Mrs. Grover's wimpy boys running back from the city at her call, and Charlene puts down the cup of coffee on top of all the loan stuff and swishes her silky hair and starts giggling, and then I can't help laughing my head off too. Then Jenny stalks in in her duct tape skirt to see what's going on and stands there looking cynical and freaked out. Mom says, "Nice skirt, Jenny," between gasps of air. Jenny's face opens like a notebook, and you can see her deciding whether to stalk off in anger or join in. But Charlene pulls her to the floor and starts tickling her, and soon Jenny starts laughing too.

By now Mrs. Grover is stalking across our backyard, ostensibly looking for Humphrey, but you know she's coming to see what all the laughing is about, because no-one in mourning should be laughing like that. It's unseemly. So she's striding across the lawn, and Mom sees her through the window, and for a second everyone's quiet. But Charlene starts giggling again, and Mom says, "Meatloaf anyone?" and pretty soon we're all laughing so hard that no-one even hears her banging on the door.

Tamarind

Anushree Varma

The tamarind tree is a sombre creature. Twisted and gnarled, its trunk sprouts a mass of long, brownish pods that hang down gloomily, like the hair of a woman who has long since been neglecting herself. Despite delicate, green filigree leaves that the slightest wind ruffles, it is the mourner among trees. But unlike the willow that tosses with such passionate longing, the tamarind is heavy with sorrow only for itself. And so what a surprise its fruit is, so tartly sweet and sour that it wakes up the most weary and jaded of tongues.

Tamar-i-hind, from Arabic, meaning date of India.

One such tree, spreading dark, cool shade about itself like an oasis, grew near the Shiva temple that rose, stony-cheeked and ancient, by our house. "Why your grandmother built the house so near a temple, I don't know. It's bad luck to live in the shadow of a temple–" muttered pruney old Vedantika, her check sari tied up between her twiggy legs as we hurried to the temple courtyard. "Why isn't it good luck to live near God?" I asked, looking up at her, but she didn't answer. She never went inside the temple. The bald priest would stop her, standing at the door and crossing his arms sternly over his bare chest covered with prayer necklaces. So, instead, we pulled off some of the dusty, crackling imli pods to carry home. We stopped only when a mottled grey chameleon scuttled close by, eyeing us beadily. It looked like a scaly, ugly snake trying to raise itself up, out of the boiling dust.

Later that afternoon the sun was greedily turning everything within its grasp to fiery, burning gold: the leaves, the houses, the gates, and the road all melted into one another. The occasional passer-by on foot or bicycle roofed himself with a newspaper held up to the side of his head. My shelter was in the kitchen, where I sat shaping birds and beasts from a lump of leftover dough that Vedantika had pounded out. Now she was straining the reddish tamarind pulp, tugging away the rough hairs with which the sticky fruit lashed itself together.

While shadowy others rustled about me, I sulked, quietly plucking out the long quills and pricks of humiliation that the morning had left in me. Earlier, when the park fires across the street were still smouldering as the gardeners there boiled their tea-water, Armaan and I had been playing in our own garden. There, among the baby cauliflowers, we'd shrugged off all our clothes – on a whim. He'd suggested it, but I was just as curious to see how he was made. Of course we'd both seen the pot-bellied brown children running about naked in the smelly squalor of the juggis nearby. But we'd momentarily forgotten that; or it may have been that we thought that the poor, though made by the same gods, were made by different parents, and so cast in entirely different moulds. Naked, the top halves of his and my body were the same – waist-high in the sea, we would have looked like twins. But our eyes were drawn to that part of each other that lay between the thighs, as distinct from one another as night from day. He looked at the shadowy folds of my body, not yet knowing that its secrets, like those of a close-lipped rose, hid within. Bolder, I reached out to hold his penis that seemed to look towards me, lifting it to see the pair of grapes beneath.

To someone further away, we must have looked as if we were bathing in the green shrubs, surrounded by colourful flecks of dahlias, fountains of green, moping grasses. It was only when Shrimata, come to dump the pail of dirty washwater, stepped closer that she saw what we were doing. Letting out an earsplitting scream like a siren, she brought mothers, fathers, and the rest of the household jamboree thundering down upon us. Some laughed, others didn't; but all eventually made angry faces, glaring masks as scary as the carved ones that Africans wear in their war dances.

Our jemadarni wasted no time in spreading news of my scandal to the other houses where she worked. Suddenly I found myself to be a pariah, at the eye of a storm of sidelong glances, whispers, and muffled laughter. Gossip, I'd found out, is the only poison you can carry on your own lips to hurt others.

Later, as the red ashes of dusk began to settle, there was another outburst of wailing voices. But not the birds' voices, thronging into the dark breasts of the trees. Singing raucously, they'd left one tree silent: the tamarind tree outside the temple, where from one of the branches the body of a man was swinging from a rope. A blood-coloured sun shone through the leaves, partly blinding me. A stranger climbed up and cut the rope with a knife, while others below held the corpse and laid him down with his head in a crying woman's lap. She was shrieking at him to wake up. People streamed in, their shocked faces piling up around us like dark, billowing waves, rising higher, until the world beyond was eclipsed.

The sardarji next door later relayed the saga. The boy in the tree was the dhobi's son, Manav. Talat, the tailor's son, had hanged him. At the bazaar, Talat had seen his sister Heena laughing and talking to Manav as he bought her some glittering red glass bangles. Spying on them, Talat discovered that they were in love. The day after, he and his cousins – stoned from smoking bidis – convinced each other that family honour was at stake. Pouncing on Manav while he was bringing bedsheets back to our colony, they went too far in their beating. Realizing that they'd killed him, they'd frantically strung him up to the tree so that it would look like suicide. But the body was so bruised that no-one was fooled.

After telling us this, the sardarji turned to shamble home, his dog panting at his side. Highly pedigreed and costly, Polki had been his pride and joy until it was discovered that he was a fake, not a purebred at all, but a loutish mongrel. Now, when they circled the block, it was with gazes turned away from each other. Under his red turban, the man's face was glum, disappointed yet again, and the dog's was somewhat guilty, as if he'd known all along that he was a gyp.

Talat was put into jail so far away that his parents couldn't visit. Once when they did, his mother came back crying all the way, as distraught as Manav's mother had been when they'd pulled her son down from the tree like some strange, dark fruit. The last we saw of Heena was when we peered down through our back window to see her embracing her family goodbye. She was beautiful as always, in her dark green wedding dress embroidered with glimmering gold threads, her arms and hands covered with fresh henna. But there was something ghostly about her, and she didn't weep as most leaving brides did. "But why so soon?" asked my mother. Shrimata answered by patting her tummy, adding, "He's from the Gulf. Rich." But he didn't look it, fat and in a rumpled suit. "What will he say when he finds out?" asked Mira, my eldest cousin, but no-one answered.

Soon enough, all of us children were clambering into the tamarind tree again, into the harsh embrace of its branches, tearing off the pods to eat the pulp. The shiny, square seeds we spat out into our palms. They became stones in the new games that the knotty-haired urchins taught us how to play, drawing a web on the road with chalk that the rain was already coming to lick away.

CUTTING

Harold Hoefle

On the table lies her note. *Eat all the food that's in the pan on the stove. I went shopping. Don't go out. There's something important to tell you. Love Mom.* The note is likely weeks old and has been left whenever she goes out, just as the food has been made daily and later eaten despite my failure to appear. I hold up the note. She has pressed heavily with her pencil, as if the thick lines of the message will ensure its commands are obeyed. I'm not sure if the missing comma in *Love Mom* is intentional.

Walking down the hall to my room, I notice that her bedroom door gapes open. I smell perfume, hairspray, starch; in the pebbled light I see scarves hanging from her mirror's frame, and on the dresser small bottles crowd a wooden box. Nestled inside are black and white photos I bring to the window's last light. I find a family portrait taken on my only trip to Austria: a row of men in dark suits and women in floral dresses, their children clamped in place by hands on shoulders. In the foreground, a white-haired man sits and dandles a baby boy – my mother's father and me. Behind us and separated by a thin space, my parents stand slightly sideways. The adult smiles cannot hide the embarrassment of country people in a formal moment. I slide the photo beneath the others and thumb through laughing girls clasping one another's waists. The last photo shows a young woman dancing past a sofa, her head tilted and black hair cascading behind her, her eyes and mouth shut, her white arms sleek in a sleeveless dress. Scrawled on the picture's back is the familiar handwriting: *Wahrstett, 10 Februar 1945.* Turning on the bedside lamp, I hold the photo to it and look at the mark on her neck, the long welt running along the side of her throat to the underside of her chin. *A dog scratched me when I came to Canada* – that's how my mother explained her daily scarves, worn to cover most of her neck. But she came to Canada in 1951. I stare at her scar, her lie, and in my mind I hear a cry, then recall the real cry I heard the last time I came home from Viv's downtown apartment. A month ago. My twenty-first birthday, celebrated the usual way: with criticism, swearing, threats on both sides, and more.

A car wheels into the driveway; I go to the front door and raise the window blind, then watch her pull the garage door open with one hand. Dressed in a yellow blouse and white pants, her blue scarf caught in her own breeze, she carries four bulging bags of groceries up the walk. I open the door and note her tight lips and the grey roots of her dyed black hair. When I hold out my hands to help her, she averts her eyes and bustles past, the bags grazing my legs. She's pushing her pain into my face, as ever, and I feel the old anger wiring my nerves.

"Have you eaten?" she says. "Everything's on the stove. Sit down, and I heat it up."

She flicks on the kitchen light, and the glare hurts my eyes. After turning on the stove's front burner, she puts some groceries into cupboards and then goes back to the stove and removes the pan's lid. With her wooden spoon she stirs the food, then stops and unpacks more bags. I know the cupboards and cold-room already have enough meat and canned goods to feed two people for months, but maybe that's the point: when you survive one war, you get ready for the next.

Her back is turned to me as she adds salt to the food. "When did you get home?"

"An hour ago, I guess."

"I bet you still don't have a job."

"I'm going to apply again at your factory for the security job."

"You stupid, they fill up positions in April! I told you to apply *so* many times." The way she draws out the *so* makes me want to punch her. I did once, when I was sixteen. A shot to the shoulder that crumpled her against a wall. For the next three days she'd confront me and roll up her sleeve, showing me the purple puck-sized bruise.

Now she pours a glass of milk and puts it beside me. "You're going back to school."

"I might."

"Might? I give you everything, and you do nothing."

Our talk is bowling down the old worn lane, and soon the pins will smash and fall. No-one ever wins, and the explosion lingers: first in the kitchen, then in my head after I leave. Departures that last for weeks while I hole up at Viv's.

I try to stay calm, keep my voice even. "Mom, in the war you were at your mother's the whole time, right? What happened?"

For a second she stops stirring.

"Terrible things. Why?"

"Were you hurt? I know the soldiers came into villages– "

The crackle of frying food fills the air, interrupting me. She's lifted the lid, and with her spoon she pushes the carrots, mashed potatoes, and chicken slices onto a plate. When some food spills onto the stove, she swears in German, then brings me the steaming meal.

The small mountain of food smells delicious. After a month of Viv's vegetarian meals, I miss meat. I start eating. I just want to enjoy my mother's cooking, not try to rip some awful truth out of her. But the thought of stopping now bothers me even more.

"Who came to your village – the Russians?"

Her eyes are on my fork as I raise browned chicken to my mouth.

"We called them Cossacks." She goes to the sink and starts to wash the pan. "Don't talk about it."

My mouth's full when she brings me a napkin, folding it as she approaches. Her hair swings slightly as she walks, veiling the parts of her neck the scarf has left exposed. I can't ask about her scar.

"Where's my package?" I say. She had called me at Viv's place that morning, saying that a package had arrived from Europe.

My mother laughs – a happy laugh, a laugh without malice – and her mouth reveals a gold tooth. I put down my knife.

"What's so funny?"

"Finish your food. I tricked you!"

Her usual manoeuvre, using lies to control me.

She leaves the room and comes back with a marble cake. A thick slice with vanilla ice-cream appears on a dish beside me, and before I can ask she tops up my glass with milk.

Her voice hits me when, my plate clean, I push back my chair and stand.

"Will you stay tonight?"

I don't answer. Answering is impossible, as is looking in her direction, so I just turn and walk down the hall.

At the front door I pause for a long minute, then I flick on the porch light and go outside. The garage door groans when I tug. I switch on the inside light and uncover the lawnmower, unscrew the gas cap and tilt the tank into the light. Low. I get the plastic-green gas container, adjust the nozzle, and fill the tank. With a rag I remove grease from the tank's lip, then make sure the spark plug's tightly screwed in. Gently, I turn the mower on its side and with a sharp stick scrape away the dried grass stuck to the hubs and the wheels themselves.

Front lawns are shining under porch lights and street lamps. Before I pull the mower's cord I look at all the houses around me: all quiet, all their windows lit.

Aline Marie Lemay

She recognizes him. Yesterday she saw him with shoulders drawn against the cold, standing outside her metro, where trampled snow becomes slush becomes muddy water. She remembers his grey wool overcoat, unevenly buttoned, and how he rocked mechanically from side to side. His hand was out, collecting melting snow and small coins, framed in a cuff so ragged it looked to her as though his fist had pushed through a solid piece of fabric.

Today, she knows it is the same person, even without the coat and the cuffs. She had dropped change into his palm, there in front of the metro, and when he lifted his head, she saw his face. Every line seemed pulled by anger, held there, cast in cold contempt. That one glance had stayed with her all the way home.

Now, at the homeless shelter, he is standing on the other side of the kitchen door. It is one of those two-part doors seen on children's television programs – the ones with the top half always open – where visiting puppets and neighbours appear from the waist up. She dries her hands on a dishtowel, brushes back a strand of hair, and faces him over the narrow ledge. He is her height, and she judges him to be about her age. His eyes do not move.

She does not smile; it would seem a trite response, like offering a bright balloon to someone about to throw himself off a building. "Hot dogs today. That okay?"

"What else?"

"That's it for the hot meal." She gestures toward the spread of salads and sandwiches in the common room. "And all the usual cold stuff if you're still hungry."

He does not turn his head, but continues to stare at her. "Nothin' but hot dogs." His voice is low, and his words run into and over one other. She has difficulty understanding him.

"And the other stuff," she says. Her eyes drop to the tattoos, blurred by excess ink, which cover his arms.

"Gimme four."

"Three. Just three per person."

No response. She hesitates, then prepares a plate of three hot dogs and holds it out to him. When he does not reach for it, she sets it on the ledge near his elbow. He squashes the hot dogs down with an open hand. "They're cold," he says, wiping his fingers on his pants.

"Really?" Frowning at the plate, she puts it in the microwave and retreats to the sink until she hears the last of the beeps, indicating it is ready.

Steam and the smell of cooked meat rise from the plate. "There you go." She puts it down in front of him.

"Gimme a cup," he says.

She reaches down for a plastic mug, but when she straightens up he is gone, taking his plate over to the condiments at the salad table. She leaves the cup out for him and returns to the dishes. Moments later, she hears the bang of plastic on the ledge behind her. Once. Twice.

She turns around but remains at the sink. He says something.

"Pardon me?" She shakes the water off her hands and comes to the door.

"Coke."

"No soft drinks tonight. Only on weekends. Sorry."

He does not stir. The cup strikes the ledge one more time. She takes a cloth and wipes the already spotless countertop until she hears the scrape of a chair pulling up to one of the Formica tables. Then she looks up. He is not far from her, head down and eating alone. She tosses his unused cup into the sink, and leans on the kitchen door.

The shelter is a windowless church basement painted chalk

167

blue. At the far end of the room, over a dozen guys watch and shout at the television, seated on chairs of metal and vinyl arranged in classroom rows. It must be an important hockey game; in two years, she has rarely seen the pool table inactive. Closed offices – where the social workers are now meeting – line one side of the room, and armchairs cluster along the opposite wall. Young men sit at tables in twos and threes, filling the air in front of the kitchen with the smoke of cigarettes rolled from leftover butts. Those unable to stay awake until the dorm opens at nine p.m. are wound into their coats, deep in the armchairs closest to the wall.

He approaches again. She quickly slides her elbows off the door ledge, which he takes over like a shared armrest in a cinema. "Where's my cup?" he says.

She puts a different one on the ledge, and he grabs it, taking it over to the juice cooler. When he passes by, she looks away, staring at the day-chef's note.

"Dessert: Use up freezer cakes." She had forgotten.

She digs out the two remaining cakes from the bottom of the deep freeze. By the time she has gathered up bowls, a tray, and a knife, he is leaning in the kitchen door again.

He says something, too low and quick for her to understand. "What?"

He repeats himself slowly, as though speaking to a child. "Why didn't I get any dessert?"

"I just pulled it out." She does not look at him. "I haven't even cut it yet. You … can have a piece." With the first cut, the knife drops and clangs on the cement floor. Chocolate icing splatters. She curses loud enough for him to hear.

She rinses the knife at the sink but does not bother to dry it before cutting back into the cake. The first piece that she lifts out, the corner piece, she eases into a bowl and hands it to him.

He looks at it but does not take it. "Bigger."

Taking the bowl back, she then cuts a second piece and shoves

168

it in next to the first. Her arm jerks when she hands it to him. He takes it from her. After dividing up the rest of the cake into servings, she wipes up the counter, the floor, and her jeans and brings out the tray of bowls.

She stays in the kitchen for the remainder of the evening. Normally she eats with the staff or the guys, but tonight she barely has an appetite for dessert. He is always on the other side of the door.

"Matches."

She hands him a book.

"Popcorn."

"Isn't any."

"Thread, I need thread."

She does not bother to sit down.

"Gimme a needle."

She is already holding one.

"Cake."

"That was the last of it."

She checks the clock again.

"Open my locker."

"Don't have a key. Ask one of the social workers."

"What are you then?"

Stop it. Stop looking at me like I'm stupid. Aloud, she says, "Volunteer."

He blinks, missing a beat. His eyebrows lift in surprise, loosening the anger from his face. "Why?" he asks.

He suddenly swings forward into the kitchen; he had been leaning heavily on the door ledge, absently turning the knob below it, and now the door stands open. He backs out immediately. She sees he is wearing white socks provided by the shelter, because she almost runs them over pushing the door shut.

"Don't know." Her tone is flippant, but her eyes have narrowed. "Why does anyone do anything? I mean, why are you here?" She looks right at him.

He stares back at her. He is first to look away. "None of your fucking business."

He does not come back to the kitchen door. Soon after, she sees him go into the dorm for the night. Her stomach is empty, the sickening-sweet taste of icing still on her tongue.

Julia K. Rohan

Sensible shoes. That was what I noticed most about Linda, but only because they didn't fit her at all. I don't mean they didn't fit her feet, like. I mean her personality. She was as un-sensible as they come, in those days. Before she got married, I mean. Did you know I had a hand in that?

We were working together at Frank's grocery, and this one day she came in tarted up like God knows what. A micro-mini, hair-bottle blonde and teased up, and the fake nails as long and red and nasty-looking as Vampira. On her face she's got the eyeliner in black rings like a raccoon and the lipstick spread on so's it's half as big again as her own mouth. And of course she's wearing them shoes, like always. Dirt brown lace-ups with the round toes and soles like fat slabs of back-bacon. The kind that don't even look good on the grannies they was made for, let alone on a girl with bare legs up to her unmentionables.

"Not appropriate attire for the workplace," says Mr Vincent, the manager in them days. And I'm thinking, "Not appropriate attire for a whorehouse," but of course I'm not saying that to her face. He makes her promise not to wear such a getup in future, and she says she's sorry, she's only dressed up special because her "fee-awn-say" is coming to pick her up after work for a night on the town. And of course she's waving around that diamond engagement ring like she's a member of the royal damn family. Everybody knows it only come from Wal-Mart. That fella of hers – Tim Sleeth – wasn't much to brag about either, if you ask me.

So she stands there at the checkout, supposed to be ringing in the groceries, but with them glue-ons she has to punch the keys with her fingers out flat so she doesn't knock them off. Then on top of it, she's chatting up the customers like they're her long-lost buddies. And wouldn't you know, most of the people in this town is so starved for affection, they're just lapping it up like plonk.

Then in walks Ralph Gunnerson. As soon as I clap eyes on him I think to myself, "Now we're gonna see something worth talking about. Just wait'll he gets a load of who's standing at the checkout." We all knew Ralph from high school when he was voted most likely to end up delinquent, dead, drunk, or all of the above. He disappeared one day, and rumour was it was him knocked up Linda's best friend Nellie Simmons and then beat her senseless and left her for dead in the bush. Trouble was she wouldn't never admit to who it was. Like she was scared or else covering up for somebody.

Then out of the blue, he's back in town, and nobody seems to know what happened to him wherever it was he went. All we know is he come back a born-again Christian, and he spends all his time either on the job as a carpenter's apprentice or going to church. Some say, "Hallelujah, his soul's been saved!" but I say he looks like all them other Holy Rollers – like someone left them on the burner too long and the water's just about boiled away. Anyway, I could have warned Linda, I guess, but she wouldn't have been afraid. She was one of them girls who liked dangerous things. Like I said – un-sensible as all get out.

In high school, she and Ralph went steady for a long while until she broke it up. So then he took up with Nellie. Nobody really knows the truth about it, but you know these small towns. They have a way of coming up with stories when there's a hole where the truth should be.

So anyways, here comes Ralph with his 6-pack of hotdogs and buns and a squeeze bottle of mustard – and there's Linda. They see each other and just kind of freeze. Then, from where I'm hiding, I see Linda kinda flinch. And then she hides her hands behind her back. I'm wondering if she's trying to hide the fake nails – and then it hits me. Tim Sleeth! He was Ralph's best friend in school. In fact, he was his only friend. But while Ralph ended up in trouble and on the lam, old Tim surprised everybody by finishing high school and getting himself a job as a used-car salesman. Now he's partners in a big dealership out on the highway. A real success story, though, like I said, I wouldn't touch him with a ten-foot pole.

So right away I know Linda's afraid of Ralph seeing that ring, but cool as can be she says, "Hey Ralph, how're ya doing?" His face is red, and he's trying not to look at her. I'm waiting to see what's gonna happen next, and then something comes over me and I start running for the stairs. When I get there, Linda's crouching down pretending to look for something, but really she's trying to yank that ring off her finger, and it won't come. Her fake nails is popping off and hitting the floor like big red beetles. "I'll just be a second there, Ralph," she's saying as I step behind her to get to the cash register.

"How are ya, Ralph?" I ask, ringing in $1.99 for the dogs and then reaching for the buns.

"I'm good," he answers, staring at Linda's bowed head.

"Linda," I says, "could you go upstairs to my office and get me that roll of dimes I left on my desk?"

Linda moves to go, but then Ralph gets around to the end and blocks her way.

"Come on, Ralph. You don't want to do this," whines Linda.

"I heard a rumour," he said.

"Ya, well, this is a small town, Ralph. There's all kinds of rumours going around," she says, all bitchy-like, her hands stuffed into the pockets of her apron.

"Ya, well, this one says you and my old buddy Tim are getting hitched."

"That's bull. I've been out with him a few times, that's all."

"That's not what I hear. I hear you've been showing off his

engagement ring to anybody with a pair of eyes."

"Who told you that?" Linda asks, backing away from Ralph and into me.

Ralph starts moving toward us, and of course Linda's hands fly out of her pockets, getting ready to ward him off. And there's that damn ring, like a headlight on high beam.

I grab Linda and push her around behind me, and then, holding out one hand toward Ralph, I reach back with the other to grab the intercom phone.

"We don't want any trouble here, Ralph," I say.

"You lied to me," Ralph says to Linda.

"I had to! You were so crazy! You're still crazy!" shrieks Linda.

Ralph lunges forward and tries to grab at her around me, so I whack him over the head as hard as I can with the receiver.

"Ow!" he yells, grabbing his forehead and staggering back a step.

"Hey Ralph, isn't that the Reverend coming in?" I say, pointing behind him to the front door. And as soon as he turns his head, I give him a good kick that sends him into a Kraft dinner display, And then – would you believe it? – there goes Linda runnin' past me, helping him up off the floor and asking him if he's alright.

Well, you probably know the rest, After she and Ralph got married, Linda went to work in Michelle's Beauteria, washing hair and sweeping up. Her hair's natural brown now. Her makeup's toned down a lot too. Rumour these days is she's expecting, but we won't know for sure until she starts to show. She drops in to see me every now and then to see how I'm doing. She's about the best friend I've got, I guess. Anyways, those shoes seem to fit her a lot better now too, if you know what I mean.

TACOS

Damien Dabrowski

So you're laying in bed after some spectacular, fireworks-going-off-in-the-movies lovemaking, and you chuckle to yourself and she's like, what? And you're like, oh, nothing, I was just thinking about the night I first saw you. I had these great tacos, with cilantro and pineapple and everything, and I totally forgot all about you until I met you again by accident like a month later. And she's like, yeah, heh heh heh, and rolls over, and the next morning you wake up and all of the photographs have her torn out of them, and the T-Bird is gone, with some urgent-looking peel-out tire tracks in the driveway.

You ever get that sick feeling? Like climbing to the top of a roller coaster hill, and suddenly looking down, and you feel your guts back down on the ground? I have it in spades. But here's why: I'm thinking, I haven't even met this girl yet and already we're doomed to failure; what would she think if she knew I was thinking about the tacos instead of about her? Because give me a beautiful, brown-eyed girl and tacos, and the tacos win every time.

This is the thing: after I saw this girl, I had these tacos, man, I don't know how I never saw this place before; it's just this little hole-in-the-wall a couple of blocks away, but man, tacos al pastor, which is basically a heap of hot and juicy pork with spices and stuff, on a tortilla. Plus cilantro, and a hunk of roasted pineapple from the top of the spit. There's just a pineapple stuck on the top of the spit, spinning around on this huge slab of roast pork. Unbelievable. Man, seriously, these are the best tacos you ever had.

But how could I ever approach this girl? I mean, with the tacos and all? For real. If I even see her again, I mean, I could walk up and be about to ask if she'd care to join me in a cappuccino. And then she'd see, like, taco drippings oozing through my shirt where my heart's supposed to be. But, christ, we haven't even met, you know? Love at first sight? Whatever. I could try and introduce myself and tell her about the tacos and everything and maybe I'd be endearing or something, or, like, cute in a neurotic way. Women go for that, right?

But I don't know, I don't know if I could play it off like that. Normally I'd never wait for a table; I'd just go somewhere else. But I saw her as soon as I walked up and I was like, oh my god, who is this girl? So I was trying to give off that I-don't-wait-for-tables-but-these-people-look-like-they're-about-to-leave kind of vibe, because I totally had to stick around. But I couldn't have been scanning for tables 'cause the place was packed, and I'd already been waiting for, like, five minutes when she caught me scoping her.

And I'm not some soft-hearted schmuck, but as soon as I saw her I thought oh my god, she's so cute, and she looks so nice, I totally want this girl to be my girlfriend. Not the old omigod I gotta bang that babe kind of thing, but what you feel, like, after the seventh date or something: justifying your drinking buddies, changing your sheets every week in case she shows up unexpectedly – *and* the hot sex – all at once.

So when I finally get a table, I make eyes a second time as I'm walking across the place and she doesn't look away, so I'm pretty sure of something. I don't really know what, but anyway I get stuck just behind a wall. Of course there was no way I could lean over real far because if she was looking, I'd feel like a total ass; and if she wasn't looking, I'd have to just curl up and die. I couldn't even get up like I was going to the john since the goddamn bathroom was right behind me; or go ask her for a light, because why wouldn't I ask the chain-smoking suits next to me?

Anyway, so I'm trying to figure out how I can work up the

balls to go and talk to this girl, or at least go and sneak a look. Then the waiter brings me a latte instead of a cappuccino. He's all trying to tell me that that was what I ordered, and I'm like, no way man. So he realizes he can't bullshit me, and he takes this superior tone and is going on about how, hey, it's just coffee and milk buddy. Anyway, so I drink it. I was never good with uppity coffee-bar waiters, and what do I know a latte from a cappuccino? But what I was going to do, I was going to leave the little shit a one cent tip. So I drink my stupid coffee all pissed off and look at some newspaper that was left on the table.

By this point I figure that the girlfriend babe has to've already left, and I'm all pissed off anyway, so I leave my penny on the table and go to leave. So when I look over toward where she was sitting, I'm expecting to see some ugly couple or a fat lady eating cheesecake, or something, and there she is. Looking back even! Shit. Son of a bitch, here's my chance maybe, and I just left a penny on the table for the damn snotty waiter to find. I'm thinking man, I got to get out of here before he runs up and makes a huge scene, and he would have too, since the jerk was such a, like, jerk for him screwing up my order. As if I could risk looking like one of those assholes who gets off on mistreating the help, 'cause, come on, these poor peoples' wage is shit, and they live on their tips blah blah blah, right? Then I'll look like a real jerk. Or worse, lose a fight with a waiter before we've even met. So I hightailed it, basically.

But man, all the way home though, I couldn't get this girl out of my mind. I actually felt the way characters in movies do after they just fell in love: the stars are all brighter or more beautiful or something, and then they'll see a shooting star that'll mean that the love is true. But that doesn't matter anyway because I was thinking about really important stuff. Like: how I'd have to start hanging around that café from now on, and what if she was only there that day, and what am I going to I say, and how am I going to meet her if I see her again? It wasn't even *if*, it was *when*; I was totally dreaming of a brown-eyed girlfriend. But on the way, I saw this taco place, and these tacos, man, you wouldn't believe it. Hands down, best damn tacos I've ever had; You could eat like ten of them, they're so good, and they cut them to order, the guy's just standing there with this huge knife and a tortilla in his hand. Man, I'm getting hungry just thinking about them.

Janet Ritchie

As a child, I bounded onto my bed at night, believing that it was only when my feet touched the floor that I was in danger from what I could not see, what in my imagination hid beneath my bed. But in the daytime I forgot that danger. I had other fears by day.

There was the Doberman who lived next door and growled at me as I walked to school past the yard that barely contained him. I was sure that one day he would find a way to snap his leash and jump the fence. I did not believe any fence could be high enough to keep me safe from his fury.

I was afraid of Billy Sims, of his face that already, at the age of twelve, oozed with pimples, of his daily demands for my lunch or my money or both. Once I tried to hide from him in the girls' washroom, crouched on the toilet seat so my shoes would not give me away, and when I had waited there half an hour and thought it was safe to leave, he was standing, arms folded, outside the cubicle door.

I was afraid of coming home after school, afraid of what my mother would have done. Once she had painted our small apartment purple. All of it purple, the walls and everything on them. The mirrors, the photographs, the curtains. There were drops of purple paint on my bed, on the pink, ruffled bedspread she had bought in an earlier, pink phase. I was glad of the purple splatters because I hated pink, though after that day I no longer much liked purple. I had grown to hate the various colours of my mother's periodic passions, and so I had hated, sometimes in quick succession, and sometimes only after weeks or months, black and white and gold and silver, and then pink and purple.

The doctor had prescribed my mother green and white capsules that she kept by the sink and rarely took. Sometimes she would open the bottle and spill them on the counter and they would fall on the floor, where we walked on them, or lie among the growing pile of dirty dishes. Cleaning was forbidden until she had one of her frenetic cleaning outbursts late at night. Sometimes the capsules ended up in our food, and that was how I got Billy Sims to be afraid of me. I handed over my lunch, a peanut butter and jelly and lithium sandwich, and on his first bite he bit into the capsule. I told him it would make him manic depressive, and he believed me even though he was two years older than me.

I thought in those days that perhaps I would become manic depressive, or that perhaps I already was. I thought that was why my father had left, to save himself, that he could not take me with him because I was already beyond saving. He did arrange for me to visit him not long after he left, and I saw he had made a whole new life for himself with a woman named Leslie who had three sons, all older than me. I was ten and the youngest son was thirteen and already his voice was changing and he was constantly rubbing his face in search of something to shave. They had a dog, a Labrador that my father told me not to be afraid of – but I was, because it was black like the Doberman and because I was scared of everything by that time and scared of his new life with these strangers who seemed already to belong to him more than I did.

When he took me back to my mother's apartment at the end of that one weekend, he dropped me off a block away, saying it would be better if she did not see him, and he promised that I could come again to his home. I thought he meant in two week-ends, the way my friend Marianne went to her father's. I wanted to believe that he meant it when he said that maybe someday I could move there with him but that right now my mother had had a shock with him leaving and she needed me to stay with her or she would go right around the bend and have to be hospitalized.

When I was little, I did not want her to go right around the bend, but I thought she had. I learned to have no more faith in the hospital than in the fence next door, because she always talked her way out of hospital too early. No, she would say, I don't believe I am Mother Theresa, or Nicole Kidman, or Joan Baez anymore. Yes, I'll take my lithium. No, I don't believe my daughter is cursed, I don't believe the neighbours are spying on me, I don't believe my phone is tapped. No, yes, no, she had figured out the answers as though she was doing a Cosmopolitan questionnaire, and they would discharge her.

After a few discharges I stopped filling her prescriptions for lithium because there wasn't any point. I stopped calling the doctor when she made long-distance phone calls to the operator in Rome demanding to speak to the Pope, when she went to test-drive a Porsche and gave the salesman a $1000 cash deposit that was all the money I had saved from my two summers of babysitting jobs, the money that I was saving so I could move out as soon as I was sixteen.

Someone else called 911 when they saw her stripping on the front lawn of our apartment building, and when she got out of the hospital again and next went around the bend, she blamed me for that. One night she tried to strangle me, and it was her madness and not my fear that saved me. I had gone to bed believing I was too afraid of her to fall asleep, only to find as I woke to her hands around my neck that I had tricked myself by dreaming that I was still awake. She didn't strangle me because she had covered her hands with Vaseline, and they slipped off my neck when I started to struggle, before I was really awake, because her hands and their greasy feel of Vaseline were already in my dream.

I never tried to figure out the Vaseline because there was no point, none of it made any sense, her getting let out of the hospital again and again, my father leaving, me staying. I was eighteen when she tried to strangle me, and it didn't make any sense that I was still living at home when I'd promised myself I would move out at sixteen. It didn't make sense that Billy Sims was the medical student on call when I was twenty-one and brought my mother to emergency after I found her hanging from the bars on the windows in the garage of our apartment building.

My therapist says I'm angry, but I keep trying to tell him I'm afraid. That's all. I'm still afraid of the Doberman next door. It's a new Doberman, not even related to the other one that died, but it growls at me too, every time I walk by. I'm afraid to go to sleep because I have nightmares that my mother knows that when I saw her hanging from the bars, I was relieved, and it was relief, and not shock, that made me stand next to her, not moving. I was thinking how my life would change if she was really, really dead, and it was only when I heard footsteps that I cried out for someone to call 911, hoping there was still no-one there to hear.

Gladys Kinnis

They had been arguing ever since they got up that morning. Jawing, he called it.

"I don't know why it is," he said.

"Every time, we come on a trip you start jawing."

She said, "That's such a vulgar word, I never use it. I don't jaw. You're the one that jaws."

He went over to the door and looked out.

"Seems like pretty near everybody's gone. Only two cars left."

She had been sitting at the dressing table painting her nails. Now she blew on them and waved her hands in the air. The fingers, soft and pudgy, were swollen around her rings.

He came and stood beside her. "It's pretty near 10:30 now. Maybe we should go and eat." There was no answer. Instead she held up her hands, inspected her nails and began doing them over again.

He looked down at her. "I thought you put that stuff on already."

"It's not stuff. It's nail polish. If you ever paid any attention you'd know I always put two coats on."

He half-turned toward the door. "Breakfast will be over."

"I'm not hungry. I couldn't eat a thing. Not after what you said this morning."

"I didn't say anything. You're the one that did all the talking."

There was a knock at the door. It was the maid, wanting to do up the room. "I can come back," she said.

The woman picked up her purse. "It's all right. We were just going over for breakfast anyway." In the restaurant, they sat without speaking. Soon a waitress came over with a carafe of coffee.

"Good morning. You folks like your coffee now?" Her smile was warm and friendly. The man beamed, "Coffee would be real nice, Miss. That smile of yours must have brought us good weather."

The woman looked out the window. The waitress disappeared and returned with two menus.

The man was still jovial and motioned the menu away. "I'll have bacon and eggs and French toast with maple syrup. I haven't had French toast in a dog's age."

"And your wife?" the waitress asked.

"I don't want anything, I'm not hungry," she said, still looking out the window.

After awhile, she turned to him, "The way you dig into that French toast, you'd think you hadn't heard a word I said this morning. I meant every word I said."

He finished eating, then laid his knife and fork V-shape across his plate. He cleared his throat and said carefully, "If that's the way you feel about it there's not much I can say."

"I guess not." She fell silent again.

She was a plumplish woman with blond hair swept up like the beehive on top of a honey jar. She wore a tight, pink sweater. Her breasts hung heavily over the table.

The man looked smaller and seemed to sink back into the restaurant stall. His thin, gray hair was parted and brushed carefully to one side. He wore a short-sleeved, small-checked shirt.

"How come you waited until now to tell me. Just when we get started on a trip."

"Waited?" Her breasts moved forward on the table. "I've been telling you for the last thirty-five years. But do you ever listen? No. You do not."

"I listen."

"No, you do not. You never hear a word I say. You only hear what you want to hear."

He picked up his coffee cup, looked inside, set it down again. "You want more coffee?"

"Sure, go ahead and change the subject. That's par for the course."

"I just asked if you wanted more coffee."

She was silent, trailing her spoon inside her cup. Then, she started in again. "What's more, how many times have you asked me to go on a trip to the States? Answer me that? How many times?"

"I asked if you wanted to go visit Myrtle in Minnesota. You never took me up on it. You never wanted to go."

"Of course." Her voice was heavy with sarcasm. "Now we have to bring Myrtle into it. Myrtle in Minnesota. The way you talk about my sister, you'd think her name was out of some bad joke."

"I was just thinking about where she lives. It's you who never wanted to go."

"That's not true. I always wanted to. You'd never agree on where to cross over. I wanted to cross at Niagara Falls, but would you? No. It had to be Detroit."

"I said Detroit was faster from Toronto, that's all."

"Faster? It's way longer. The truth is, you wanted to visit the Ford Motor factory."

"It wasn't the factory. It was the museum."

"Whatever. Factory, museum. You had cars on the brain."

He sat with his hands in his lap.

"Everybody visits Niagara Falls," she went on. "Couples go there on their honeymoon. They get their pictures taken with the Falls in the background. But could we ever? No, we could not. Not once. We couldn't even bring back souvenirs like the Hamptons did."

"We can go there, if you want. I don't mind."

"I don't mind. I don't mind," she mimicked him. "You never mind. But do you ever show any gumption? Any git-up-and-go?

Ever say 'we're going,' just like that? *We're going*?"

"I brought you here, didn't I?"

"Well, it's about time." She fell silent, then began again. "And speaking about Myrtle, have I ever said one word against your family? Have I? They just send us their old Christmas presents, stuff they don't want, but do I ever throw that up to you? I do not." She paused, then added haughtily, "I'm above that sort of thing."

"I know you tried hard with my family." He sounded tired, as if he wanted the argument to end.

She waited, then thrust out her left hand. The red nails glowed at the ends of the pudgy fingers.

"And look at that, the diamond's so small you need a magnifying glass to see it."

"It was the best I could afford. I was only making eighty dollars a week."

"And who was doing her best to make ends meet? Who sewed new collars on your shirts, just so's they'd last? And made bread pudding week after week for dessert. You forget that."

The man didn't say anything.

"You'd think you'd want me to have a better ring after all these years, a bigger diamond."

"I got you a pinkie ring, didn't I?" pointing to her little finger. "You said you wanted a pinkie ring."

"It wasn't what I wanted. It was a new engagement ring. To show them you still cared." She began to cry. Tears flowed down her cheeks. She wiped them away with the back of her hand then rummaged in her purse for a kleenex. He handed her a paper napkin.

"Don't cry," he said. "I don't like seeing you cry."

She dabbed at her eyes and blew her nose.

"You want something to eat?" he asked. "How about a nice piece of pecan pie?" She didn't answer.

"Come on," he coaxed. "Pecan pie. How about it?"

"I don't mind," she said, turning from the window. "Order it if you want."

He motioned to the waitress. "Two pieces of pecan pie."

"You want whipped cream with that?"

"I don't mind," she said, still sounding sulky. "It's up to you."

"That'll be two pieces of pie with whipped cream." The man smiled at the waitress. "Just seems like, whenever we come on a trip, we have to have our piece of pecan pie."

He sat up straight and smoothed his hair, looked in his coffee cup and saw that it was empty. She dabbed at her eyes with the soggy napkin. He handed her another.

"There, that's better," he said. "You're going to feel a lot better now."

Marie-Andrée Cantillon

Rue Principale, rue de l'Église, rue de l'École, this is my village.

This is what my cousin Lucette calls it. "You have no avenue, no boulevard, you live in a village." She must know, she is older.

All the streets draw a bow around a column with an angel at its top. I always keep my eyes on the angel. Because his wings are open, he could fly away. If I blink my eyes very fast, I make him fly. When he is behind me, I turn so fast I spin, and I yell: " Freeze." This is why he stays.

Near the angel is the church with a very pointy hat, so sharp it could pop clouds high in the sky. From anywhere in the village, the church looks at us. This must be why mother says that God is everywhere.

Across from the angel is my favourite store. My nose sees it before my eyes do.

There, Madame Biscuit bakes cookies. At the end of the mass I kneel, but never all the way to the ground. I don't have time for it. I run in front of my mother while she talks to her friends. I race to chocolate heaven. Madame Biscuit makes the fluffiest mille feuilles – and also almond-paste pigs and frogs with chocolate bead eyes. If I have been a good girl (she asks my mother first) she gives me the longest chocolate eclair. This is why I love Sundays.

We all live in red houses. They hug each other alongside the sidewalk. Every morning, from my parents bedroom window, I see women coming out of their houses. They each carry a bucket and a mop.

The water must be warm, because the buckets spit smoke. Then the women give the sidewalk its morning bath.

Our house has two doors. One for the people who come to see my father, and one tucked to the side, just for us.

Our door is made of wood; my father's is made of glass. Everyone sees how well he works. We live upstairs. Downstairs belongs to my father.

I used to think we had two cooks in the house: my mother in the kitchen with her many pots and pans; my father with many different shape bottles – brown, green, blue. He also had shelves full of round, red and white boxes. Mother has a sink, counters, and a table. My father, too, has a sink, and also a long counter all around the room. I see him mixing spices. Hanging in front of him is a white piece of paper, a recipe – just like my mother. With his fingers he pinches the powder and lets it fall like rain into a bowl. With his hands he rolls many little round balls. He covers them with white puffball after he places them in the red boxes. My mother bakes gingerbread cookies. We call them speculoos. They are the shape of stars, trees. Mother has wooden molds; father has heavy shiny ones. He shapes "torpilles" that big people call suppositories.

There are two differences between my mother's kitchen and my father's kitchen.

My father receives money, and he has no table. No-one ever comes to sit and eat with him. He wears a white coat; mother has a white apron. I guess it is a man's thing to have a white coat, since the man across the street wears one too.

He is certainly not as clean as my father. There are red spots and lines all over his white coat. He is our butcher. Even with his many knives he doesn't scare me. What is in his window does. I never want to stop in front of it. I walk quickly, eyes closed.

They were open once. My eyes sank into those of a pig whose head was on a plate; nose up in the air with parsley in his nostrils. I prefer the pinky pigs from Madame Biscuit.

From my bedroom window I see L'Abeille, another store.

Régine Pon-Pon is a roly-poly woman. She is so much bigger than my mother. I call her Régine Pon-Pon because she always puts a round red flower in her hair. Secretly I wait for a bee to land on her head. She must too since her store is called L'Abeille. She sells food, but most of all candies in all colours, sizes, and shapes – and mountains of candies and boxes of forbidden bubble gum. I am not allowed to have any bubble gum. Mother says only cows chew. I made myself the promise that when I am old I will buy all Régine Pon-Pon's bubble gum and blow a bubble larger than my face.

My parents' bedroom is just above the pharmacy. That is what my mother told me my father's store is.

He makes people feel better. When I am in the front room, I am never allowed to make noise, run, stamp my feet, yell, or even sing or laugh.

A few days ago, so says my father (for to me it seems like a very long time), it came as an alarming surprise to hear my mother slamming doors, pulling down drawers, banging boxes. All this was happening above the pharmacy.

People were not going to feel better. The door was slightly open, and I slid into the room. Mother didn't see me. I sat on her bed. I sank into it, my feet dangling above the floor. I knew I had to be quiet, very quiet, make believe I wasn't really there.

My mother ran so fast the curtains were moving. She was packing a suitcase. I rolled my eyes all over the room, from her clothes to the suitcase, back and forth, back and forth. I tried to follow her every single move, but my eyes didn't roll fast enough. She suddenly saw me. She stopped.

"Your father is having a l-i-a-i-s-o-n with l'Abeille."

Father? l-i-a-i-s-o-n? L'Abeille? The words bumped into each other. What did all of this mean?

"I am going back to my mother."

If she was going back to her mother, who was going to be my

mother? She pulled the suitcase so strongly and so fast I thought she was going to hit the walls. The door went kaboom! For sure the house would break.

I wait watching doors, any door in the house. Maybe if I don't take my eyes away from any doors I will make her walk through one.

DEAR MS. FUNGUS

Rachel Mishira

November 11th, 2001

Dear Ms. Fungus,

What you don't get, never have and never will, is that, when everybody else is handing in their "private" Journals for M.E., this stays under the dresser where it's supposed to be. Losers. If they had any brains at all they'd all do what I do, which is hand in a bunch of other stuff about how they had a bad childhood. Or talk about how everybody else is doing drugs but they're not, and they have ambitions and dreams. Lots of dreams. I don't think you'd want to know about my dreams. They're what my journal's mostly made up of, they're no business of yours. Fuck you.

My Dad got pissed at me today. He called me a pimple, and said he'd smack me upside the head if I didn't take a hike in 32 seconds. What is it with the 32 seconds! Then he starts counting and I'm gone, no point staying around to get whacked, except I missed supper again and landed up walking all the way up the mountain. Nobody was home, or maybe they were all writing their stupid journals. Or getting clipped upside the head. Or scarfing down the food groups and sharing their innermost thoughts. They probably share their underwear, too. Losers.

I'd never seen so many stars, ever. Maybe in the country, but I didn't know Montreal had them. I lay on my back up by the Cross. It was spooky because there wasn't anybody else around. Dad says that gay guys go up there, for sex, but I didn't see any. I called Lucius on my cell. He had to tell his parents he was doing homework at Josh's house, but he drove up to the park and parked. In the parking lot of the park. And then, hehhehheh, he parked in me. Dear Ann, my boyfriend thinks he's a car. Is there anything I can do about this? Dear Grounded in Montreal, "B" is for boyfriend and you are a garage. Add a "b" to garage and you are garbage. If you don't want to be left on the curb and dumped, don't act like trash.

I like Lucius's car. He's a good driver, even if he's stoned. I never have to ask him to put on a condom, and he never makes me do anything I don't want to. I can talk to him about almost anything. When he finishes at Concordia we're going to go somewhere, like Europe, though I'd like to see where he's from in the Caribbean. I don't even know where Tobago is. He wants to go to Rome. I told him I speak a little Italian, because of my mother, but she left so long ago I don't really remember much. His name is more Italian than I am, even if I'm officially half. I don't want to go to Italy anyhow. All my relatives stopped wanting to see me after my mother left.

I saw a shooting star, too. It looked like a tracer bullet on the night-vision stuff they show on TV in Afghanistan. Like a piece of phosphorescence going across the green screen onto some tank or exploding into a cave. Thank God they don't land here.

Ms. Fungus says write about your room. What's the point. If I want to keep my teddy bear on my bed that's my business. She'd be surprised at how neat everything is. Everybody is. Lucius only comes in when Dad's at work, but he's impressed that I make my bed and put everything away. He calls it a treehouse because so much of the stuff is free, like you'd find it in the forest, walking along a path. The top of my bedside table is an extra cuttingboard from the basement. The table is a recycling box someone left out. All my clothes are in milk crates you find behind restaurants. There's so much good stuff lying around, all you have to do is take it home, or find it lying around the house. I put the postcards my mother's relatives used to send up by the mirror.

It's got to be Lucius. I only fooled around with Josh once and he didn't even put it in all the way. Dad's going to kill me. He's going to slap my whole head upside the head and put me out on the curb with the trash. I can't believe I'm pregnant. October 11th the test is positive but I knew it before that. I knew I knew it. September 11th and Josh after school watching New York get trashed by the terrorists. What was I thinking!! And then I go over to Lucius's place because his parents are out. It has to be him. I'll be showing by Christmas. Dear Ann, My life, blah-blahblah, is a mess. I'm either going to have a little black blahblahblah, or a little white blahblahblah. In either case my father is going to slap me upside the head, or kill me, or ground me for life. What should I do? Dear Dead in Montreal, There are many organizations whose sole purpose is to help unwed mothers such as yourself. Pregnancy can be a joyous experience, even though you are puking your guts out every morning and feel like the World Trade Centre. Whether the baby is black or white doesn't matter, even though neither of the possible fathers will provide support of any sort, and your own father will disown you and put you out with the trash. Remember that you have been doing aerobics and eating food groups and that even if maternity clothes look incredibly stupid, your shoes will still fit, even if you get fat ankles, and those can be removed by liposuction, which is covered by Medicare, as long as you're under eighteen and on Welfare. Go to your local Clinic for a check-up regularly, and remember to floss or you'll end up looking like your baby. Or babies – in a pregnancy such as yours, there's a good possibility of a multiple birth, such as triplets – one little white baby, one little black baby, and one little mulatto baby. Good luck, dear, and go see your Guidance Counsellor.

I don't want to see my Guidance Counsellor. My Guidance Counsellor is my Moral Education teacher. My Moral Education teacher is Ms. Fungus. I am fucked entirely. I can't go to school, I'll puke on my desk. Then I'll puke on Ms. Fungus's desk and the

Principal's desk and Josh's desk and Lucius's desk. This morning at Remembrance Day nobody saw me puke on the way to the parade but someone will see me puke somewhere and then everybody will know. I'm glad people were crying this morning so nobody noticed me crying. When the guns went off all I could think of was what was in my stomach, that the baby would get damaged by the sound, and that nobody should have to die or get shot or grow old in wheelchairs. So many names on the wall. The old lady who put the flowers down on the ground had a son who died over fifty years ago and she was still crying. One of the soldiers helped her up to lay the wreath. His knees were red where his kilt didn't cover them. Men have weird knees. When the pipers started to march away all I could think of was I want to keep this baby, I want to keep this baby, I want to keep this baby. Dad's home. Gotta go.

Day's Lee

"Two," Jingping Chen carefully enunciated and pushed a five-dollar bill through the opening in the glass. Thin lines marbled the skin across her knuckles, red and dry from washing vegetables and rice daily and cracked from the heat of gas fires generated under the giant woks. At forty, she had the hands of a woman twice her age. In her haste to change out of her splattered uniform and arrive on time at the Park Avenue theatre, she'd forgotten to slather on hand cream.

Two days ago, one of the waiters told her the theatre next door to the restaurant was showing Chinese movies every Wednesday afternoon for the summer. A Chinese movie! In China, she once walked several miles to the next village to see this marvel. Here in Canada, the black and white television images didn't make sense because she didn't understand English.

Ever since they bought the restaurant four years ago, life was a cycle of work and sleep. Overseeing the kitchen meant endless hours on her feet. Between customers arriving for breakfast, lunch, and dinner, there were chickens to kill and pluck, egg rolls to make, homemade pies to bake, and supplies to replenish. A bowl of rice, some stir-fried meat or fish, and a cup of tea was downed in a short thirty-minute lunch break. Friends commented that her five-foot-three-inch frame looked smaller since she'd lost weight. Rivers of grey seeped into what used to be ink-black hair, now cut short to fit under a hair net.

The middle-aged woman in the glass booth bobbed her Jackie Kennedy hairdo in understanding and rang in the sale. "One adult, one child," the cashier confirmed in a heavy Greek accent. "Three dollars fifty." Her plump manicured hand took the five-dollar bill and then slid the tickets and change across the green marble counter and through the slot.

Jingping picked up the tickets and tucked the change into the black vinyl handbag she had purchased at Morgan's department store the week before. "Aie-yah! Come. It will start soon," she said to Ruby in their Hoisanese dialect and headed towards the front doors with her ten-year-old daughter at her heels.

"What are we watching?" Ruby's dark inquisitive eyes roamed over posters lining the foyer walls. Some boasted unfamiliar Greek movie stars in family or romantic settings. The French posters were adorned with drawings of handsome men clutching pretty women in various states of undress.

"A good movie. A Chinese movie," replied Jingping.

"In English?"

"Mandarin."

As eager to see the movie as she was to sit down and give her swollen feet a rest, Jingping ushered Ruby into the theatre. Heavy faded curtains dominated the front of the room. The lighting was dim but not enough to hide the gold paint peeling from the mouldings and the water-stained textured wallpaper.

"Where should we sit?" Jingping scanned the sea of red seats.

Ruby shrugged and stuck out her lower lip. "Anywhere. There's nobody else here."

They made their way down one row. "Here. This one is good." Jingping unfolded a seat and sat on the thinning velvet upholstery. "The middle is good."

Then the room went black and the burgundy curtains peeled away from each other, revealing a large white screen.

"Mommy," Ruby whispered. The darkness urged her to use her theatre manners. "Do you understand Mandarin?"

"No," came the equally hushed reply. "You read the English words and tell me what it says."

After a short black and white National Film Board clip about the Antarctic, the soothing, plucking sound of the erhu signalled the beginning of the main feature. Scenes of majestic mountains, the Yellow River, and peasants working in rice fields flashed across the screen. Chinese script unfurled to a drum roll.

"What does it say?"

"The Young Warriors," Ruby read aloud. "Can you read the Chinese words on the bottom?"

"No," Jingping confessed, then quickly added. "I forgot my glasses."

A young woman and an old man worked the fields.

"That's her father," Ruby translated. "They don't have enough to eat for the winter."

The smell of ox manure and freshly plowed fields floated through Jingping's memory.

"The girl has to leave the village to find a way to make money," Ruby said after awhile, "and that boy is going too."

"You don't have to explain now," Jingping whispered. "I understand." Ruby leaned back, lifted her tiny feet onto the edge of the seat and tucked her knees under her green cotton dress.

After a tearful goodbye, the boy and the girl set off on foot. Danger confronted them along the way, but the girl's expertise with the sword saved them. With the grace of a seasoned warrior and a sweep of hardened steel, she defied highway robbers, struck down wild beasts, and shielded them from the power of angry gods. A purse of gold was her a reward for capturing thieves. Her family would have enough to eat for the winter, but the girl learned that no matter what happened, the power to take care of them was always within her.

"Mommy," Ruby peered at her through the darkness as triumphant music brought the film to a close. "Are you crying?"

Jingping took a deep breath to keep her voice steady. "No. My eyes are tired." Rising to her feet, she said in a determined voice,

"Come. It is almost 4:30. I have work to do."

Minutes later, after she donned her uniform and entered the kitchen, Jingping took her place at the butcher's block that doubled as a small table. A row of worn black handles filled the crack created by the block and the edge of the steel counter that housed dishes and cookware. The handle felt familiar and solid in her grip as she slid a small butcher's knife out of its sheath. She reached into a metal bowl containing bok choy and positioned the vegetable on the block. Then, with the swiftness and sureness of a warrior, she slashed the knife through the air, the iron blade rhythmically tapped the wood underneath.

Robert Davies

Giuseppe Cavalacchio, known to his friends, enemies, and customers alike as "Pep," parked his four-door, pink 1965 Cadillac Eldorado right outside his office on the corner of St. Denis and St. Catherine streets, got out, and began to work. His office was literally the corner itself, a zero-rent location where for one hour each day he held court, lent out money at ten percent a week, took collections, threatened delinquent debtors, and received supplicants. The Montreal landscape wasn't as attractive as his native village near Naples, of course, but there was a lot more money to be made in the New World, and Pep took as much advantage of the propitious business climate as he could. The pink Caddy was his trademark: he got it on the cheap off a tardy borrower, an art dealer who had bought the car after seeing Salvador Dali tooling around the Spanish resort town of Cadaqués in just such a vehicle. In fact, there was a certain surrealism in seeing the Italian mobster cruising the streets of Canada's metropolis in such an easily identifiable car. It was art – well almost – but also a tribute to just how well Pep was connected. There was more than enough vig in his cash flow to cover off the payments to Montreal's finest, the cops and prosecutors on the "pad" who studiously ignored the Italian's usury and strong-arming of any unfortunate borrower who couldn't trek down to Pep's corner for the weekly interest payment.

For a number of months just after I turned thirteen, I got to see Pep and his exotic car every week, because my father, unable to convince a bank to fund his business, was a regular user of Pep's individually tailored financial services plan. It wasn't exactly "freedom fifty-five," you know, more like "eternal servitude," but since my dad had a high line of credit with Giuseppe Cavalacchio, he was absolved from having to trudge over to Pep's downtown street-corner office for deposits and withdrawals. We got door-to-door service. Of course, since my dad was always late paying, Pep would frequently drive down from his house in the northern Italian enclave of St. Leonard at any and all hours of the day, always unannounced, and ostentatiously park right in front of our Westmount home – to my mother's evident chagrin. After waiting for a few minutes to let the tension rise, so to speak, he would exit his car, stride up the walkway, and bang noisily on the front door, loudly cursing my father all the way back to the steppes. Looking for his delinquent client, he would bellow at my mother, Helen: "Where's your effing husband, Madame?" There was always an excuse, of course, "out of town" being the usual, always followed by a threat, to which my mother never in fact seemed to pay much attention. The threats were usually accompanied by a shaken fist and a promise to return in the middle of the night for more vigorous collection efforts. And always, when he came by for his envelope, there was that iridescent pink Cadillac, which was to my teenage mind the symbol of Pep's power and of his hold over our family.

One autumn afternoon, as I returned home from a particularly gruelling high school Latin exam, I cringed to see the Caddy parked again right in front of our house, but then I blinked and did a double take as I realized with astonishment that the driver's side door was gone. Not just wide open, mind you, but completely missing!

Pep was talking to my mother on the stoop, accepting an envelope with a partial payment that had somewhat mollified his ill humour, and apologizing for the foul language he had employed in his last telephone conversation with her. "You gotta know, Madame," he was saying as I came up the stairs, "I should'na spoke to a lady that way, but I was brought up rough, and your husband, well, he gets me mad he's always late with the payment. You gotta tell him to treat me wit' respect."

"Never mind that, Pep," she replied, "but tell me, what happened to the door of your car?"

A flurry of expletives ensued as Pep railed at some evil kids who were certain to suffer a terrible fate if he ever found them, street punks who had stolen the door during the previous night while the car was parked in front of his luxurious marble-faced residence. Also cursed roundly was General Motors, who even back then couldn't get a replacement part without bringing it in from Binghampton, Skokie, or Cleveland. "They all robbed me, Mrs. S. At least two weeks, Madame, I'll be driving wit' no door for at leas' two weeks. Everybody gonna laugh at me now!"

The missing door was the subject of much gallows humour at our dinner table that evening, my father having materialized from his hiding place just in time for the tasteless, pallid, over-cooked kosher steak that was a family staple. We imagined the burly mafioso cruising the streets of the east end, cursed by the need to make his collections in that now laughable automobile. His customers were sure to demand an interest rate rebate, at the very least!

But two days later, when Pep returned to our home, un-announced as usual, seeking my father, looking for more money, I peeped out the window of my second-floor corner bedroom and saw to my amazement that the car was whole again: the pink door was back in its rightful place. I crept quietly down the large circular staircase that led to the ground-floor hall and overheard the following exchange:

My mother: "What happened to your Cadillac, Pep? The car dealer get lucky?"

This brought a deep chuckle from the mobster.

"Well, you know, it's the funniest thing, Madame, a friend of mine found another car just like mine out in

Laval, same year, same model ..."

My mom: "So what? I don't understand."

Pep: "Well, Mrs. S., let's put it this way. My car is OK again, and that other guy, in Laval? Ah, the door is *his* problem now."

That was the last time I saw Pep. I think he gave up on lending money to our family out of respect for my mom, who told him he would end up having a heart attack if he kept on dealing with my father. Surely there must be plenty of easier customers he could find? So much the better for our family. But in a funny way, we all missed him, savage threats, gesticulations, and all. And as for me, well, for years after that, despite myself, every time I saw a pink Cadillac Eldorado cruising the streets of Montreal, I would instinctively crane my neck, just to see if the driver's door was firmly attached to the car.

ABOUT THE WRITERS

Suzanne Alexakis is a mongrel Montrealer who began knitting words together while on walkabout in the South Pacific. She has (so far) published poetry and prose in literary journals and anthologies overseas and in Canada.

Patrick Allard's "A Moment Near Solo" is his first attempt at creative writing. He has been travelling, running away from himself for the better part of twenty years, and hopes that through his writing he can make sense of his journeys. He is 33 and currently teaches English in Taiwan.

Matthew Anderson holds a doctorate in New Testament from McGill, lectures at Concordia's Dept. of Theology, and is a parish pastor of the Lutheran Church. He has published academic non-fiction, devotional and opinion pieces, and some poetry. A Playwrights' Workshop/CBC radio drama competition chose his script "The Deer" as one of five winners.

Connie Barnes Rose is the author of *Getting out of Town*, a collection of linked stories. She has also published stories in a variety of journals and anthologies and is currently wrestling with her first novel.

Marla Becking is from Snow Lake, Manitoba and now lives in Montreal. Her short story "For all my Relations" was short-listed for the Canadian Authors' Association Developing Writers Award in 1997 and won the David J. Walker Prize in Creative Writing at the University of New Brunswick in 1998.

Angel Beyde writes and edits in Montreal. She is currently working on her first novel, *The Tasmanian Devil*, of which "FlipFlop" is an excerpt. Her fiction has appeared previously in *Prism* and *Prairie Fire*, and she is a contributing editor for *Matrix*.

Andy Brown is co-editor of *You and Your Bright Ideas: New Montreal Writing* (Véhicule Press). This story is from a forthcoming book *Looking for Parking* (Conundrum Press).

Marjorie Bruhmuller lives in the Eastern Townships of Québec. Her poem "A Fine Line" was published by the Townshipper's Association in 2000, and her short stories have appeared in *Flood Quarterly*, local newspapers, and on the CBC. She is a member of a creative writing group and is working on a cookbook for celiacs.

Marie-Andrée Cantillion was born in Belgium, raised in Africa, and thirty years ago chose to live in Québec. She studied creative writing at Ryerson and the Victoria School of Writing and is a psychologist and tour guide. "Abracadabra," a short story, was published in the Clifden Writers Group Anthology in 2001.

Frederic (Nick) Carpenter is, primarily, a writer for the stage, and his work has been performed in Montreal, Toronto, Calgary, and Chicago as well as on CBC radio. His short story "The Pattern" was a winner in the 2001 Commonwealth Broadcasting Association Short Story Competition. His current play *Stained Glass* is being developed through the 2001/02 National Arts Centre Playwrights' Unit.

Damien Dabrowski lives and writes in Montreal. He rarely eats tacos there.

Eric James Dallow was born in England and moved to Montreal in the eighties to escape Thatcherism. He has worked in a wide variety of professions and is presently enjoying a mid-life sabbatical while he takes stock of his moral, political, artistic, and spiritual values.

Robert Davies is a well-known Canadian publisher of books in English and French, and is co-author of a series of mysteries for teenagers featuring K.C. Flanagan, girl detective. He is presently completing a novel about the intersecting lives of a Frenchman, a French-Canadian, and an American Jew.

Norris Domingue was born in 1925, a Cajun from Louisiana, and spent three years in the US Marines. He attended the University of Texas, then spent two years with Ringling Brothers Circus. He has been a busboy, bellboy, merchant marine, ballroom dance instructor, singing waiter, clown, stand-up comic, filmmaker, and actor.

Liam Durcan lives in Montreal. In the last year his work has appeared in *The Fiddlehead, Grain, Zoetrope All-Story Extra, The Paumanok Review,* and *Absinthe Review.*

Linda Dyer balances her life as a business school professor with her interests in literacy and fiction writing. She has previously published a story, "Temp," written for the adult literacy learner.

Ian Ferrier is one of the core poet/performers in the North American performance literature scene. *Exploding Head Man, jazz poems* a CD and book was published recently. He can be heard on CBC, public radio stations in the US, and on Canada's NCRA college stations.

Marisa Gelfusa entered the CBC/QWF short story competition to gather the courage to put her writing out into the world. Simply pushing the envelope with her story into the mailbox was her main objective. The rewards for taking the risk have been startling and wonderful.

Harold Hoefle teaches English at John Abbott College. He has published fiction, travel writing, and reviews. His short story "Czechs" will appear in *Front & Centre.* He is now reviewing for *The Danforth Review* and *Books in Canada* and nearing completion of his first short story collection.

Gladys Kinnis is a former social worker who was, for several years, the moderator of a seniors' short story writing group at McGill. She wrote her first short story at six and resumed writing after her retirement. She is presently working on a novel and a collection of short stories.

Day's Lee is a graduate of the Journalism Program at Concordia, where she also studied fiction writing. She has taken courses offered by the QWF. Her publications include articles in *Rice Paper Magazine,* and *Canadian Living,* as well as fiction in the *Fit to Die Anthology* and *Story Teller Magazine.*

Aline Marie Lemay, born and raised on the Prairies, has been living in Montreal since 1989. She is currently enrolled in the Creative Writing Master's Program at Concordia and works as a freelance copywriter and museum planner/experience developer.

J.G. Lewis, a late bloomer, returned to university after years as a blue collar worker, to graduate at 40 with a BA in creative writing. *A Date With Lily* is the first story by the author ever submitted anywhere. It took 53 years to submit this one. The author hopes it won't take another 53 to submit the next one.

Colin MacWhirter is a writer and artist who was born in Alberta and has lived in Montreal since 1990.

Julie Mafood has completed several creative writing courses and workshops and been part of a writers' group everywhere she has lived during the past 11 years. She has had work published in *Public Works Magazine*, *The Jamaica Daily Gleaner*, *Friendly Erotica*, and *The Antigonish Review*. She has performed her work at venues around Montreal. This is her first published short story.

Lelia Marshy spent a few years in Cairo once upon a time not so long ago and now lives and works in Montreal. Her poetry and short fiction have been included in numerous journals and anthologies.

Celia McBride is a Yukon-born writer and theatre artist whose plays have been produced in Montreal, Toronto, Ireland, and Paris. Her one-act play "Walk Right Up" will be produced at the Stratford Festival in August 2002. She is part of the Writers' Lab at Factory Theatre in Toronto and a graduate of the National Theatre School of Canada.

Neale McDevitt is a thirty-eight-year-old Montrealer who, despite moving nine times, has lived in the same four-block radius his entire life. A former member of the Canadian National Weightlifting Team and a recently retired rugby player, he is finding that writing is much easier on his knees. He has won several writing competitions and appears in a spoken work open mic show, "Wednesday's Child."

Ken McDonough is a local translator who has lived in Montreal for the past 15 years. Thanks for reading my story. Peace.

Rachel Mishari is an anagram.

Lauren Kathryn Morgan graduated from Bishop's College School in 2001. She has had work published in *Inscape* and *First Fruits*. She won the British Commonwealth Essay Prize, the first Canadian to do so.

Susan Motyka, a native Montrealer, was the recipient of the 2000 Irving Layton Award for fiction for her story "Blind Drive Right" and is currently a graduate student in the creative writing program at Concordia.

Earl Murphy is a graduate of the School of Architecture at McGill and has been involved in such projects as Habitat '67, Pollack Hall and UQAM's School of Design. He later studied watercolour art and creative writing and began writing full time in 1996. He is currently writing his first novel.

Elaine Kalman Naves was born in Hungary and grew up in Budapest, London, and Montreal. She is a literary columnist for *The Montreal Gazette* and the author of four books, including *Journey to Vaja: Reconstructing the World of a Hungarian-Jewish Family*, which won the 1998 Elie Wiesel Prize for Holocaust Literature and has been made into a documentary film. She is currently working on the sequel.

Mark Patterson is a Montreal writer whose fiction has appeared in *Blood & Aphorisms*, *sub-TERRAIN*, *Broken Pencil*, and the *Fruits of the Branch* anthology. He is host and producer of the Grimy Windows Variety Showcase, which features prose, poetry, comedy, music, film screenings, and wrestling.

James Rae has created short stories, original photo books, poetry and film scripts. He does copyediting and translation and has been a professional actor in film and television in French and English for almost two decades. He is also a photographer and short-film director with exhibition and publishing credits in Canada and abroad.

Janet Ritchie's "Peanut Butter and Jelly and Lithium" is her first published work.

Emma C. Roberts graduated for the English and creative writing program at the University of Windsor and then studied playwriting at the National Theatre School of Canada. She has won several prizes, and is currently a member of the 2001-02 Tarragon/Chalmers Playwrights' Unit in Toronto.

Kirsty Robertston is a PhD candidate in the department of Art History and Communications Studies at McGill. She studies the visual culture of protest movements and the importance of national identity, cultural difference, and multiculturalism in the world of Canadian art exhibitions. This is her first work of fiction, and she plans to continue writing.

Julia K. Rohan divides her time between Montreal and the Eastern Townships.

Jeremy Stafford lives in North Hatley, and this is his first published story.

Anushree Varma lives in Montreal. She studied literature and comparative education at McGill and received the Pearson Prize for Poetry and the Shapiro Award for Creative Writing while studying there. She teaches modern languages at a local CEGEP and often returns to India, her birthplace.

Sarah Venart has lived in Montreal since 1996. Her work has appeared in *Matrix, Prism, International, sub-TERRAIN*, the *Antigonish Review, ribsauce, Headlight 4*, and *A Room at the Heart of Things*. She is currently focusing on her first novel, *Now We Know Who to Hate*, and a poetry manuscript, *Tea Leaves Are Little Windows*.